JESSICA COLE
MODEL SPY

Also by Sarah Sky

Jessica Cole: Model Spy: Code Red Lipstick

JESSICA COLE
MODEL SPY
FASHION ASSASSIN

This is a work of fiction. Names, characters, places, incidents and events are products of the author's imagination or are used fictitiously. Any resemblance to actual people, living or dead, events or locales is entirely coincidental.

www.scholastic.co.uk

SARAH SKY

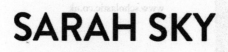

Scholastic Children's Books
An imprint of Scholastic Ltd
Euston House, 24 Eversholt Street,
London, NW1 1DB, UK
Registered office: Westfield Road, Southam, Warwickshire, CV47 0RA
SCHOLASTIC and associated logos are trademarks and/or
registered trademarks of Scholastic Inc.

First published in the UK by Scholastic Ltd, 2015

Text copyright © Sarah Sky, 2015

ISBN 978 1407 14018 6

A CIP catalogue record for this book
is available from the British Library.

Printed by CPI Group (UK) Ltd, Croydon, CR0 4YY
Papers used by Scholastic Children's Books are made
from wood grown in sustainable forests.

1 3 5 7 9 10 8 6 4 2

This is a ... ...
and dialog... ... ...
fictitious ... ...

For Mum, Dad and Rachel, with love.

PROLOGUE

The ghost was back. The pink diamond chandelier earring slipped from Madison Matthews' fingers. She froze as a chill descended on her dressing room. It was deathly silent, but someone or something was watching her every move and waiting.

She'd sensed a strange presence hours earlier, right here in the most luxurious penthouse suite of Los Angeles' Beverly Wilshire Hotel. Her stylist and jewellers had been helping her try on the seventy million dollar necklace everyone was talking about; five platinum chains embedded with twelve thousand pink diamonds. The piece had been designed especially for her to wear tonight. Judging by the faces of Stryker, "Team Madison" and the security guards, she'd upstage every other female nominee on the red carpet. They wouldn't stand a chance against her diamond armoury.

Ker-chang!

But an unwelcome visitor had also arrived. Madison was naturally intuitive about these sorts of things; her life coach and spiritualist always said so. It was as if someone had opened a window; she'd felt a cool draft as she touched the glittering stones around her neck and caught a brief flash of something in the corner of her eye. A vague, blurry shape shifted and then disappeared like fine mist into the curtains as her make-up artist, manicurist, eyebrow technician and publicist huddled around her. They'd scared it away in the nick of time, whatever it was.

Now she was alone and it had returned.

Goosebumps pricked her arms and her heart hammered against her ribcage. It must have drifted closer. She felt breath on the nape of her neck, strange eyes burning into her exposed back. It was directly behind her, reaching out. A hand grabbed her. It didn't feel like a ghost. The fingers were warm, and hard nails squeezed into her skin. Her knees almost buckled beneath her.

A silent scream formed on her lips.

"You look hot, babe!" Stryker nuzzled her neck as his arms tightened around her waist. "The paps are going to love us. We'll make the front pages tomorrow."

"It's you!" Madison steadied herself against a chair. She'd never been so relieved to see her boyfriend. She could taste blood in her mouth. Had she bitten her lip? Fumbling in her make-up bag, she dug out a diamond-encrusted compact. She *had* nipped her lip but it was easy to cover up with a slick of pink gloss. She blotted her face with porcelain powder but the perfectly applied make-up couldn't disguise the fear in her blue eyes.

"Of course it is, babe. Who else would it be?" Stryker laughed, then struck a pose into the full-length mirror across the room, running a hand through his spiky highlighted blond hair. He hadn't noticed that her hands were shaking.

Madison shrugged as she smoothed her long blonde locks behind her bejewelled ears. He'd laugh if she told him. He might have a super-fit body, but he was the

3

least spiritual person she'd met. *Ever*. And that was saying something in a business that was full of super-shallow people.

"We need to leave now if you want to rock the red carpet, babe."

Did he have to keep calling her "babe"? He said it at the end of every sentence. Was he always this annoying or were her nerves super frazzled today? She was seriously freaking out. If she won all eight nominations tonight, she'd make Grammy history at the age of nineteen. But Gretchen X might scoop best female artist instead.

Stop it, stop it, stop it.

She had to keep calm. She'd come too far to have *her* gong snatched away by a talentless little girl who was barely out of high school.

She turned and fixed her most dazzling smile at Stryker. He stared open-mouthed at her shimmering pink Azzedine Alaia gown, hand dyed to match her diamonds. She'd known he'd like the plunging neckline. He looked hot in his black Armani suit. Pity they couldn't have a proper grown-up conversation that didn't involve how many press-ups he'd done or which vitamin shakes tasted best.

Madison shrugged. "Give me a minute. *Babe*."

"OK, babe," Stryker said, missing her sarcasm. He turned to leave, stealing one last glance in the mirror.

"Wait!" she called after him. No way was she being left on her own again with the Ghost of Suite 619. As she bent down to scoop her earring from the carpet, she thought she saw it again in the corner of her eye, shifting and gliding towards her.

"Let's get out of here!"

"Sure thing, babe. Let's rock this party!"

She grabbed Stryker's arm and fled, banging the door shut. He could forget nipping off to the bar to chat up some fawning model-slash-actress while she was pressing the flesh with music execs.

If he left her side once tonight, their relationship would be history.

"And the winner of Best Female Artist is. . ." presenter K-2 grinned as he slowly opened the envelope.

This was it. Madison had won all her categories so far, but this was the big one. Best Female Artist. She smiled at Stryker. The camera pointed directly at her, waiting to capture her reaction. To her left, the security guard sat stony-faced. He hadn't left her side all evening, even when she went to the ladies' room. He'd been under strict orders from the jewellers to watch over the necklace. She hadn't sensed the ghost at the ceremony. Maybe it couldn't leave the hotel room? Trapped for ever in an afterlife of five-star luxuries. There had to be worse places.

"Gretchen X!"

The starlet rose to her feet, a vision of shimmering crimson.

"NNNNOOOOOOOOOOOO!" Madison leapt up and staggered into the aisle.

"It's mine! *Mine*! You can't have it!"

The auditorium fell silent. Gretchen X stared, open-mouthed.

"What the…? Sit down, babe!" Stryker attempted to grab her. "Everyone's watching!" He fixed a grin on his face as the camera zoomed in.

K-2 coughed nervously. "Er, OK, then. Let's have a big old round of applause for Gretchen X!"

The ripple of clapping faded out.

"Give it back now!"

"For the love of God, babe, you're embarrassing yourself!" Stryker slumped into his seat, hiding his face behind his hands. "And *me*."

Madison spun around. "Where are you? I know you're here. Give it back!"

"What are you talking about?" Stryker whispered. "We're so over, babe. I've been meaning to break up with you for weeks."

"Stop calling me 'babe'! I'm talking about the necklace! It's gone!"

The security guard leapt up, speaking urgently into his headset.

"We have a lockdown situation here." He grabbed Phoenix Saf, who sat behind Madison, and dragged him to his feet. "I need to search you, sir!"

"Get your hands off me!"

"Where's the necklace?" the security guard growled.

The rapper threw a punch, catching the guard on the corner of his mouth. Within seconds, a full-scale brawl erupted live on TV as pop stars, music execs and various hangers-on joined in.

In the pandemonium, Madison was sure of two things. First, she knew that the ghost had stolen her necklace, not Phoenix Saf. She'd felt its chilly fingers around her neck as it ripped off the diamonds before disappearing, will-o-the-wisp like, into Grammy history.

Secondly, she knew she'd never get nominated for Best Female Artist again.

CHAPTER ONE

"Where is it?" a voice hissed in Jessica's ear.

A figure crouched beside her pillow in the darkness. She awoke in full panic mode and hurtled out of bed. She lunged for her diamanté key ring; it fired an electric current that would poleaxe her attacker instantly, no problem.

Dammit.

It fell off the bedside table, along with the lamp, but she felt her Gucci sunglasses beneath her fingertips. Fumbling for the hidden switch, she activated "night vision" and slammed the glasses on.

"You!" Jessica exclaimed.

The glasses revealed Katyenka Ingorokva groping for the light switch on the wall. Suddenly, the room was illuminated, blinding Jessica. She whipped off her glasses as the fourteen-year-old Russian supermodel spun around, scowling fiercely. Katyenka tossed her jet-black hair over her shoulders, her green eyes sparkling with anger. Jessica squinted at her black leather Jean Paul Gaultier bustier and skirt that showed off her endless legs. Going to bed wasn't real high up on this girl's agenda.

"Where have you hidden it?" she demanded.

"Hidden what exactly, Katyenka?" Jessica put her sunglasses back on the bedside table.

Her room-mate from hell had no idea what a lucky escape she'd had. If she'd found her key ring before the sunglasses, Katyenka would be unconscious in the back of an ambulance by now.

"How many times do I have to tell you? My name's Kat, not Katyenka, and I know you've got it."

Jessica picked up the dented lamp and alarm clock. It was one a.m. Kat was the pits. They were sharing a hotel room during a shoot in New York for a spread in *Miss Mode* magazine. It was turning out to be one of the longest weeks of her life, and that was saying something considering she'd survived three murder attempts this year. She wished she'd been able to persuade Primus to break the rule that models had to share a room.

"What have I hidden this time, *Kat*?"

"My diamond earring, of course! I put it on my dressing table and now it's gone."

"Is that the same diamond earring you left next to your toothbrush earlier? Have you bothered to look in the bathroom before accusing me again?"

Honestly! Kat kept dumping her earrings in the stupidest places – she'd left them in an empty coffee cup, along with a stubbed-out ciggie, during Tuesday's shoot, and under a magazine on the concierge's desk yesterday. Without fail, she accused someone of stealing them, but they always turned up. They were hard to miss – the diamonds were practically as big as her fist.

Kat strode into the en suite and emerged sheepishly a few seconds later, twirling the glittering stone around her fingers.

Jessica touched her ear. "Did I hear right? Was that an apology?"

Kat shrugged. "Someone in my position can't be too careful, you know."

"Er, right." Seriously? Did she mean her position as the most self-centred brat in the whole universe? If only Jessica had found her key ring first!

"Why were you sleeping in your sunglasses, anyway?" Kat smirked as she tossed the earring on to her dressing table. "You Americans are so strange."

How many times did she have to tell her? "I'm British, remember? And—"

Jessica stopped herself in time. She couldn't possibly tell Kat that the glasses were a gadget; a present from her dad along with the key ring that could also crack safe combinations. He wasn't big into gifts of clothes or make-up. That's because he wasn't like most other dads: he was a private detective and a former MI6 agent.

"Maybe I'm a little strange," Jessica finished.

She could hardly deny it. Her whole family was odd by most people's standards. They were all spooks, or former ones anyway. How weird was that?

Kat snorted. "Hello? You're *big-time* strange."

She flounced off to rummage through a towering pile of discarded designer clothes. Handbags, shoes and dresses flew across the cream carpet. A stiletto narrowly missed Jessica's thigh.

"This might sound like a silly question, but what are you doing exactly, Kat?" she asked. "Do you have a sudden urge to donate some clothes to charity?"

"Ha ha. You Americans are funny *and* strange. I'm looking for my strappy gold Armani top. Have you seen it?"

"Er, no, but isn't that the Louis Vuitton handbag you lost yesterday?"

"This?" Kat held up the cream clutch. "I don't want it any more. It's *so* last season. You can have it." She tossed it on to Jessica's bed, along with a designer black bra. "Take this. It'll give you better support."

"Gee, thanks."

"You're welcome. I'll also give you a hundred dollars if you help me find my top. I'm going to be late."

Jessica rolled her eyes. Kat had an annoying habit of treating her like an employee, and that was when she was in a good mood. When she was in a temper – which was about ninety-five per cent of the time – she treated people like her personal slaves.

"I think I'll pass this time," she said. "But late for what, dare I ask?"

"Some hot guys I met earlier invited me to the opening of a new club. Aha!"

Kat pulled out a miniscule gold halter-neck top from the clothes mountain, making it topple over.

"You're going out now? You are joking, aren't you?"

Kat whipped off her top and shrugged on the halter neck. She pulled out a black-and-gold embossed business card from her cleavage and waved it at Jessica. "You can come if you want, but I'd probably have to lend you something to wear."

Hmm. That was Kat's code for saying she didn't own any clothes that made her look like a pole dancer. She'd take that as a compliment.

"I'll pass, thanks. We've got to be at the shoot really early tomorrow. Who are these guys anyway? Do they know how old you are?"

Kat erupted into fits of laughter. "Who do you think

you are – my mother? I don't need one, thanks. I'm doing fine on my own."

Jessica flinched. "No, but—"

"I can do whatever I want," Kat interrupted. "Ask any of Papa's ex-girlfriends or my nannies. They can't control me and neither can you."

Kat shoved her feet into a pair of gold-studded Alexander McQueen peep-toe sandals, which made her tower over six feet tall, and grabbed a matching knuckleduster clutch, which was embedded with glittering jewels. She tottered to the mirror to apply her scarlet lip gloss. Jessica stared at Kat's illicit packet of ciggies and lighter, next to her Swarovski-encrusted mobile. Smoking was bad enough, but heading off in the middle of the night to hook up with men she'd just met was crazy.

But so what if Kat wanted to go clubbing with total strangers who might turn out to be complete psychos? Sure it was beyond dumb – dumber than smoking – but it wasn't *her* problem. She stared at the lighter again. What if something awful happened to her, and Jessica could have stopped it? Kat clearly couldn't look after herself.

She edged closer, pretending to look at her discarded designer clothes. "Is that from Chanel's last catwalk show?" She pointed at a green-and-white striped dress, screwed up in a tight ball.

Kat sniggered. "Don't you know anything? It's vintage Christian Dior, of course!" She darted towards her mobile as it beeped. "Hilarious! Raoul is so cute and funny."

As she texted back, Jessica swiped the lighter and fled to the bathroom, using it to set fire to a corner of *Elle* magazine. The smoke alarm screeched almost instantly.

"What the hell's that?" Kat yelled.

Jessica quickly doused the magazine with water in the sink and returned to the room, shaking her head. "Beats me." Triggering the alarm would land them both in a lot of trouble but she couldn't think of another way to stop her.

"I can't stand this racket. I'm outta here!" Kat grabbed her ciggies from the table and frowned. "Where's my lighter? It was here a minute ago."

"Don't you know how bad smoking is for you?"

Kat's eyes narrowed. "Do you have it?" She lunged

16

at Jessica, wrestled her arm from behind her back and snatched the lighter from her fingers. "You did this! You cow!"

Kat spat out a string of Russian swear words.

"So what?" Jessica said. "I can do whatever I want. You can't control me."

"I'll get you for this!" Kat spluttered with fury as the door banged open. She quickly tossed the lighter back to Jessica.

A grey-haired woman, wearing a blue dressing gown, flew into the room. It was their dragon-like chaperone, Annette. Hot on her heels was a suited man whose name badge identified him as the hotel's duty manager, Mr Burt Tanning.

"What's going on in here?" The stockily-built man swiftly inspected the suite before pulling up a chair and deactivating the smoke alarm. He clocked the packet of cigarettes on Kat's bedside table as he stepped down.

"We have a strict no-smoking rule in this hotel. You should both know that already." He glared at the girls. "Who's responsible for this?"

"Let me guess." Annette's eyes roamed disapprovingly over Kat's outfit. "I warned you I'd report you to your agency if I caught you smoking again. Two strikes and you'll be hauled back home."

"It wasn't me, honestly." Kat scowled at Jessica. "Miss Goody-Two-Shoes had a fag in the bathroom. Look, she nicked my lighter."

Jessica glowered back. She made a mental note to add "sneaky telltale" to Kat's long list of character defects. "I'm sorry. I was messing around with the lighter and it triggered the alarm. It was an accident. It won't happen again."

"Make sure it doesn't," Mr Tanning barked, "or we'll ban you both from this hotel." He stalked out, shaking his head.

Annette stood her ground, arms folded. "I'd expect this kind of stunt from Kat, but you should know better, Jessica."

"I know, but—"

"This is your second chance already," Annette interrupted. "Don't blow it. You won't get another one."

The words stung Jessica into silence. She nodded.

Kat glanced from one to the other, puzzled. "What did—?"

"I don't want to hear another word from either

of you," Annette said sharply. "You need to be at your best tomorrow. You can't let down the client or Primus, so take that make-up off right now, Kat, and get to bed. You too, Jessica."

Jessica felt herself redden as Kat slunk away to the bathroom.

"I'm disappointed in you, Jessica," Annette said as she walked to the door. "I really am."

Join the queue. She wasn't exactly winning a Miss Popularity contest at Primus right now.

She climbed into bed and felt for her late mum's pendant around her neck. Staring at the ceiling, she rubbed the locket between her fingers. She'd been thinking a lot about her mum recently, and she was missing home. Eight days away felt like for ever. If only she were back in London, hanging out with Becky in their favourite coffee shops in Ealing and hunting for vintage clothes at Portobello market in Notting Hill.

Things had started to hot up with Jamie, the coolest, best-looking boy in school, too, before she flew out to New York. Now they'd be apart for most of the summer holidays, what with her working and him gigging with his band and travelling with his family, and she had no idea how serious they were. Were they even officially going out?

The bathroom door swung open, interrupting Jessica's thoughts.

"What did Annette mean when she said you'd already had a second chance?" Kat asked. "I'm curious. What have you done? Taken drugs or stolen a designer gown? You don't look the sort, but you never can tell."

Jessica looked up. Kat had changed into pink silk pyjamas. With her face scrubbed free of make-up and hair tied into two long plaits, she looked much younger than fourteen. Kat rearranged the collection of Harrods teddy bears on her bed and climbed beneath the pink silk covers that her dad had shipped over from Paris.

Jessica flicked the light off. "I've no idea what she was talking about. Go to sleep."

"Whatever."

She buried her face in the pillow as Kat's MP3 player blared to life, pumping out Kesha. There was no point telling her the truth – that a woman called Margaret Becker, a treacherous MI6 double agent, was hell-bent on ruining her life. After failing to kill her, she'd attempted to derail Jessica's modelling career by blackening her name in the press.

Kat wouldn't believe her story. Who would?

CHAPTER
TWO

"Higher! Higher! Again!"

Sebastian Rossini bellowed orders as Jessica bounced on a trampoline. They'd been at this for hours. With every leap, she struck a new pose to make it look as if she were sailing effortlessly above the New York skyline, from the top of the Flatiron Building, at the junction of Broadway.

Her legs felt like jelly and her stomach was churning horribly. She was so high up, the yellow cabs were just dots on the street below. It gave her flashbacks to a recent modelling shoot when a safety wire had been sabotaged and she'd plunged six storeys from the top of a building; saved only by an MI6 bracelet that contained a hidden super-strength nanowire. That experience hadn't helped her fear of heights.

Stop looking down.

Thanks to Kat, she'd only had a few hours' sleep and couldn't focus properly. It must be close to forty degrees Celsius, yet she was wearing a long black leather Armani trench coat and biker boots – perfect on a winter's day, but not for one of New York's blistering summers. That's what happened when you were always shooting a season ahead; you ended up wearing bikinis on freezing winter beaches in Devon and woollen jumpers and cashmere coats in the scorching Sahara desert.

"One last time," Sebastian ordered. *"C'est magnifique!"*

Jessica kicked her legs high in the air. She'd sworn never to work for Sebastian again after his last photo shoot involved being stuck underwater with a giant snake for hours on end, but she couldn't afford to turn down work when her dad was so ill in hospital. Someone had to pay the bills now his multiple sclerosis had worsened. He wasn't well enough to take on any new cases, and she had barely modelled since first getting entangled with MI6 six months earlier.

Back then, Jessica had nearly been killed by a deranged former supermodel, Allegra Knight, who had tried to release a face cream that would deform thousands of girls. To make matters worse she'd joined forces with MI6 double agent, Margaret Becker, and a terrorist called Vectra. Allegra and Vectra had escaped from the police and were still at large. Margaret Becker had got off scot-free after framing Nathan Hall as the double agent – a fellow MI6 colleague who also happened to be Jessica's estranged godfather.

Soon afterwards, stories were leaked to newspapers that falsely claimed Jessica had sabotaged the launch of the face cream due to her involvement with animal rights activists. She was convinced that Margaret was behind the damaging lies – the first step in a vicious campaign designed to discredit her. Her modelling assignments dried up and her agency couldn't get her a single go-see, let alone book a show, because designers feared attracting damaging headlines. Overnight, Jessica became a fashion pariah. Most of the bookers at her agency, Primus, still refused to take her calls.

Sebastian had proved an unlikely saviour. He'd been massively impressed by their underwater shoot for *Mademoiselle* magazine and wanted to work with her again. Jessica was as surprised as everyone else when he insisted she was the only other model he'd shoot for the four-page New York spread in *Miss Mode*, alongside Kat. Word had spread that she was "in" again, and offers of work were trickling into Primus.

Sebastian gestured for her to climb down from the trampoline. Shakily, Jessica eased herself on to the ground, which pitched and lurched beneath her boots. She steadied herself against the railing and peered into his digital camera. *Wow!* She was flying above New York, like some kind of glamorous anarchist. Her strawberry-blonde hair was scraped into a tight bun and her eyes were sprayed with black paint, making the sparkling diamonds in her ears and around her neck appear even more luminous.

"That's what I love about you, Jessica," Sebastian said, smiling. "You always deliver, no matter what I throw at you. *Très, très bon.*"

Kat pouted as she fiddled with her large diamond-encrusted platinum cuff.

"It's *so* not fair," she whined. "Jessica has the best clothes and jewels. That's the only reason she looks better than me."

Jasmine, the head stylist, overheard and rolled her eyes at her team. They'd had enough of Kat's childish strops, which had been going on all morning.

"You both look *très jolie*," Sebastian insisted. "You're my stars of the future. Look at your photo, Katyenka. It's stunning."

He flicked up the pic on his camera. He was right. It was an amazing shot. Kat looked like a diamond-encrusted goddess.

"See, Katyenka?"

Kat pouted but didn't dare correct him about her name. "Not bad, I guess." She folded her arms as an assistant dragged Sebastian away.

"I told him I needed more jewels," Kat muttered, "but he wouldn't listen." She held the glittering diamond cuff up to the sun. "Do you think Sebastian will let me keep this?"

Jessica laughed. "Haven't you noticed the security around here?" She nodded at the group of Armani-suited men, clutching mobile phones. They hadn't taken their eyes off the girls all morning, and they were in addition to the beefcake bodyguards who stuck to Kat like glue each day.

"Every piece has to be accounted for, Miss," one of the Armani security guards said, stepping forward. He clutched two large red cases. "We don't want a repeat of the Grammys or the Frick museum, now do we?"

"What do you mean?" Jessica stretched her arms out as Jasmine and her team stripped her of jewels, placing them carefully in the cases.

He pulled out a copy of that morning's *New York Post* from his jacket and handed it to Jessica. She scanned the front page.

THE GHOST STRIKES AGAIN!

Detectives are baffled by the theft of a valuable porcelain from the Frick Collection in New York which "disappeared into thin air" yesterday.

Visitors and security guards claim that an eighteenth century pot-pourri vase was snatched from a table in the Fragonard Room at about eleven a.m. – by a "ghost".

Police admit they don't know how a thief could have removed the porcelain from the building in broad daylight without being detected.

They are questioning all visitors and members of staff and have refused to rule out an inside job.

A source at the museum said: "Several visitors and security guards claimed the vase suddenly vanished, yet nobody was nearby.

"Despite a lockdown and search of visitors as they left the building, nothing was found."

The baffling case has echoes of the Grammys raid, when actress Madison Matthews was robbed of her seventy-million-dollar pink diamond necklace during the ceremony, live on TV.

Ms Matthews claimed the necklace was unclasped by a "ghost" who'd been stalking her. She remains in rehab, recovering from her ordeal, and has split from Hollywood heart-throb Stryker Daniels.

"Oooh, I love a good ghost story." Jasmine grinned as she unfastened Jessica's necklace.

"There has to be a rational explanation," Jessica replied. "Maybe—"

"Where's my cuff?" Kat shrieked. She clamped her hand on her wrist. "It was here a minute ago and now it's gone. It's the ghost! It's struck again!"

"No way!" exclaimed Jasmine.

"Way!" Kat wailed. "It's gone! I swear!"

Everyone stopped and stared, open-mouthed. Even Jessica's heart beat a little quicker. It couldn't be true. Could it?

"I think I can solve the mystery." One of the guards bent down. "It seems to have slipped in here."

He pulled the cuff out of Kat's cream, quilted Chanel handbag.

"How did it get in there?" She smiled innocently and batted her long spidery lashes at the guard.

Yeah, right. As if she didn't know.

"I'll take it now before it gets lost again, Miss," he said stiffly.

Kat shrugged. "If you must."

"You should be ashamed of yourself pulling a stunt

29

like that," Jasmine muttered, as the guard stalked off with the jewels safely packed away. "It gives models a bad name when jewels or clothes disappear on a shoot."

"It was an accident," Kat protested. "I dropped it. Anyway, I own much more expensive things than that little trinket. Papa bought me seven-million-dollar pink diamond earrings for my birthday, you know."

Jessica stifled a yawn. Kat was unbelievable. All she talked about was how much her papa spent on this and that. But after today, who cared? Someone else would have to put up with her twenty-four-seven showing off.

"I'm going back to the hotel to pack," Jessica said shortly. "Are you coming?" *Hopefully not.*

Kat snorted contemptuously. "I have a maid who packs for me. I've got Papa's credit card and I'm going to buy a whole new wardrobe before I leave New York. Everything I own is so tired and *sooooo* last season."

Jessica stifled a giggle. She'd never heard clothes described as tired before. That must mean her wardrobe – a mix of Topshop and vintage bargains – was completely exhausted.

"Good for you. I'm flying back to London tonight and won't see you again."

Fingers crossed. Everything crossed. She wouldn't miss Kat the brat one little bit.

"How tragic," Kat said in her worst English accent *ever*. "Did I tell you I'm going to Papa's yacht in Monaco?"

"Only about a million times. Oh, make that a million and one." Jessica walked towards a tarpaulin tent, which was being used as the changing room. Kat had been rabbiting on about Monaco, and how her dad owned one of the biggest, most expensive yachts in the world, to anyone who'd listen for days now.

"By the way," Kat called after her. "Did your boyfriend ever bother to text back?"

Jessica caught her breath. There must be lots of reasons why Jamie hadn't messaged yet. He was probably busy preparing for his gig. He was a really talented singer and guitarist, and might even attract a record company scout if this summer went well. There was also the time difference to figure in. Plus, maybe he was rehearsing in a basement that was a mobile phone black spot. Ignoring Kat, she strode towards the tent. Phew. She'd almost made it.

"Thought not!" Kat gloated triumphantly. "He must have met someone else. Can't say I blame him."

Jessica shoved her feet into her favourite pair of tan gladiator-style sandals. She'd scrubbed off her make-up and thrown on a white vest and denim cut-off shorts. It was too hot to dress up. Her black nail polish looked odd in summer, but she'd remove it at the hotel; anything to avoid having to spend another minute near Kat, who was still crowing about Jessica's boyfriend – or rather lack of one.

She messaged Jamie again in the lift.

Flying back 2nite. Can't wait for yr gig tomorrow xxx

Then she sent texts to Becky, Dad and her grandma, Mattie. Her dad and Mattie messaged back straight away, but there was nothing from Jamie or Becky. Was Kat right? Had Jamie found someone else? Was that why Becky had been keeping radio silence for the last couple of days as well? Maybe she didn't want to be the one to break the bad news to her and was waiting to tell her face to face. Jessica's mind raced with a million and one different scenarios, none of which had a happy ending. Hopefully it was all in her head, which was feeling pretty fried by the blazing sun.

A blast of humid air smothered her face like a giant woolly blanket as she stepped out on to the street. Cabs tooted their horns loudly and workmen drilled and yelled. *Whoaa!* Jessica halted, momentarily stunned. Living in London, she was used to constant noise and buzz, but it was nothing compared to this. A shiver of excitement travelled down her spine. This is what she'd missed most when she couldn't book a single modelling job; nothing beat the thrill of being in a new city. No other job gave her the same independence and opportunities to travel. She was lucky and she knew it.

"Miss Cole? Over here. I've been waiting for you." A handsome blond man wearing a black suit and peaked cap stepped out of a white limo and waved. "I've been booked to take you back to your hotel. I can't wait much longer. I'm parked illegally."

Cabs hooted as they were forced to overtake the limo. A cyclist flicked a rude gesture. New Yorkers certainly didn't hold back.

"Geez, give me a break!" the driver shouted after him.

"Oh, sure. Thanks." She hadn't expected a lift –

she'd been riding the subway back in the stifling heat all week – so this was a nice last day treat.

"Let me help you with your bag." The young man grinned, flashing a set of perfect white teeth. He took her large blue Mulberry handbag, a thank you gift from Sebastian, and opened the passenger-seat door.

Jessica sank into the black leather seat; it was deliciously cool. She mopped her forehead and the back of her neck with a chilled wet tissue and fished out an icy bottle of water from the same compartment. So this was how the other half lived. A chauffeur-driven limo was clearly the way to travel in New York. The car purred to life, and she stared through the blacked-out window as they glided past clothes boutiques. If only money weren't a problem, she'd be hitting the shops right now.

Unfortunately, she couldn't afford any mementos from New York, except maybe a miniature Empire State Building key ring for her dad. He loved the nineties movie *Sleepless in Seattle*, where Meg Ryan and Tom Hanks finally met on top of New York's landmark building. He watched it again and again. It was hilarious seeing a hard-nosed former MI6 agent, who'd been involved in countless dangerous missions, be reduced to a blubbering wreck by a fluffy chick flick.

Yes, she'd definitely look for a piece of tourist tat. It would cheer him up.

What was the driver doing?

"You're going the wrong way." She banged on the partition. "The hotel's downtown."

The glass blacked out.

"Hey!" She pounded on the partition again. "Didn't you hear me?"

Jessica tried the door handle but it was locked. She grabbed for her mobile and remembered the driver had taken her bag as she got in. It was on the front passenger seat.

She started to panic. She'd got into a car with a total stranger and hadn't demanded to see his ID. He could be anyone.

She'd let herself be kidnapped. Her dad had trained her how to avoid this exact kind of situation. How could she have been so dumb?

CHAPTER
THREE

Jessica shivered violently as the air conditioning ramped up to full blast. Goosebumps pricked her arms. She was such an idiot. She'd been so distracted by the buzz of New York, a cool ride and freebies that she'd forgotten her dad's rules. *Notice everything. Question everything. When in trouble, do absolutely anything to get away.*

That was one of her dad's rules she'd definitely obey. She pulled a small retractable nail file from her shorts pocket and clenched it tightly in her fist. She'd be ready when the limo finally pulled over. A sharp jab to her kidnapper's throat or face would give her vital seconds to escape.

She glanced out the window again. If the driver

planned to attack her, why were they still in such a public place? He could easily head to some deserted car park or wasteland outside the city, but instead they were snarled up in traffic, with plenty of eye witnesses milling around.

The car eventually pulled up outside the Waldorf Astoria, one of Manhattan's most exclusive and luxurious hotels. The partition window peeled down and Jessica sprang forward, gripping her nail file, but the driver's reactions were quicker. Without turning around, his hand shot up and grasped her wrist.

"Drop it!" he said. "There's a good girl."

Jessica cried out as he squeezed harder. He was going to break her wrist. She let go. "You'll regret—" she began.

"Someone's waiting for you on the Starlight Roof, eighteenth floor," the man drawled.

"Who? What are you talking about?" She rubbed her throbbing wrist.

"Go see. I'm only the chauffeur."

He leant over the partition, dangling her handbag. She snatched it off him and rummaged inside for her mobile. Found it! She looked up. "Kidnapper's a more accurate job description."

"If you say so, Miss Cole."

"You can forget it. I'm going back to my hotel." Jessica tried the door handle. It swung open, engulfing her in noise and heat again.

"That's up to you, but you'll need to hail a cab. My shift's over."

She jumped out, clutching her mobile. "Your shift involved abducting me. I'm going to report you."

The driver laughed. "Be my guest. I'll be long gone by the time the police turn up – *if* they turn up. 'Girl chauffeured to Manhattan's best hotel for a surprise lunch' doesn't strike me as an emergency situation."

He waved his hands in mock horror. "Help me, officer, help! I didn't like the free, delicious lobster or oysters."

Jessica slammed the door and memorized the number plate as the limo pulled away. She was *so* going to report him. She looked up and down the street. Typical. Not a single yellow cab in sight. She'd walk a few blocks to calm down. Her pulse was racing like mad – she could feel blood pumping through every vein in her body.

She took a few paces and stopped.

Wait. Why should she calm down? How dare someone do this? Who did they think they were? She had no idea who was responsible, but she was going to find out. She was confident she'd be safe in a public area, surrounded by diners. This would be one lunch they'd never forget. Hopefully they'd choke on their lobster or whatever it was they were eating.

She doubled back, marched through the hotel reception, ignored the concierge, and leapt into a lift as it closed. An elegant, Chanel-clad woman recoiled as she took in her fraying denim shorts and black nail polish.

The door pinged open on the eighteenth floor. The woman sashayed out first, leaving a cloud of expensive perfume lingering in the air. Jessica followed her through the marble rotunda to the dining area. The manager beamed at the Chanel woman as he checked her booking before she was led away by a glamorous blonde waitress.

"Can I help you?" The manager's eyebrow shot to the ceiling as he looked Jessica up and down.

"I'm here to meet someone," she replied. "By appointment."

"We have a dress code, Miss," he said icily. "No shorts allowed. You'll have to dine elsewhere today. There's a McDonald's a few blocks away."

"Yeah, well I've got a no-kidnapping code, so go figure." She folded her arms, challengingly. He didn't want to mess with her today. "I'm not going anywhere and I'm certainly not going to McDonald's."

"And your name is?" the manager said, transfixed by her black nail polish.

"Jessica Cole."

The man jumped. "Miss Cole? I'm so sorry. Come this way. Let me show you to your table. The other member of your party has already arrived. Please follow me."

Today was getting more weird by the minute. She walked past vast displays of cream roses and ice sculptures of swans. Winged horses leapt across the gilded ceilings that dripped with exquisite crystal chandeliers. Heads turned as they made their way through the restaurant. The Chanel lady sipped champagne. Her eyes widened as she clocked Jessica.

40

Keep your hair on, lady. She wasn't stopping. She'd see who was at the table and yell at them; Mattie called it the "hairdryer treatment".

The manager stopped and gave a little bow. "This is your table. I hope you enjoy your lunch, Miss Cole. Please accept my sincere apologies again for the mix-up."

He stepped aside, revealing a lone figure sat at the table. The blood drained from Jessica's face. Her knees weakened. The chatter of voices, the clink of cutlery and the aroma of freshly baked bread melted away into the background. She stood, statue-like, unable to tear her eyes away.

"Margaret Becker," she said finally. "You have to be kidding."

"You should know by now that I never joke. Take a seat, Jessica. We need to talk."

Her pulse raced. Margaret was a traitor to MI6. Using the alias "Starfish", she had ordered Allegra Knight to kill Jessica and her dad six months earlier to prevent an illegal deal with Vectra from being scuppered. She'd even set up Jessica's godfather. She hadn't changed that much since the last time they'd met. She always wore a silk Liberty scarf knotted at her throat; this one was patterned green and grey to match her grey jacket. White hair curled around her ears that were studded with large creamy-coloured pearls. To any onlooker, she looked like a kindly grandma treating her granddaughter to a special lunch, not a ruthless double agent. They probably wouldn't notice the icy steel in her grey eyes; the hardness that signalled she was prepared to do anything, *absolutely anything*, to get what she wanted – including killing anyone who got in her way.

"You look well, Jessica." She smiled sweetly. "However the nail polish is a tad Goth for someone my age. Is it Chanel or Nails Inc.? It's so hard to find one that doesn't chip after a day or two, don't you find?"

Jessica shook her head in disbelief. She didn't trust herself to reply. Margaret was acting as if nothing had gone on between them. Her eyes strayed to the knife on the table. It was tempting to use it on her.

Margaret's hand stretched over and covered the knife. She stared back, unflinching. She was untouchable and she knew it. Nobody at MI6 suspected she was lying. Why would they? Margaret had incriminated Nathan very convincingly; she'd made sure that every illegal act she'd committed was traced back to him. He'd been badly hurt when Allegra blew up her beauty headquarters, and he was still in a coma, unable to clear his name. The doctors had told her dad that he was unlikely ever to wake up.

"Why on earth would I want to have lunch with you?" Jessica said finally. "Pretend all you want to everyone at MI6, *Starfish*, but you don't fool me. You ordered Allegra to kill my dad and me – not Nathan."

Jessica watched her closely. Margaret didn't even flinch. She was as cool as the ice sculptures. Cooler even.

"That's a very serious accusation." Margaret calmly took a sip of chilled white wine. "I'm curious. Do you have a shred of proof? Because I'd love to hear it if you do."

"You know I don't or you wouldn't be sitting there," Jessica said loudly. "You'd be locked up in prison where you belong. Do you think your beloved grandchildren will want to visit you when you're finally behind bars?"

Margaret's mouth twitched slightly as she placed her wine glass down.

Yes! She'd hit a nerve.

"Your comments are slanderous, and I could sue you as they've been overheard." She nodded at nearby diners. "However I understand the terrible stress you and your family have been under recently. Despite everything that's happened, I was truly saddened to hear the doctors' prognosis for Nathan."

"Oh, please!" Jessica scoffed. "It's much more convenient for you that he never recovers. He'd be able to expose you if he did."

Margaret shook her head slowly as she lined up her cutlery. "At some point, you'll have to accept the truth that your godfather is Starfish. You believed it too, remember? Back in Paris you were certain of it."

"You tricked me into suspecting Nathan. I regret doubting him. But you've got a lot more on your conscience than me, remember? Exactly how many innocent people have you killed over the years? Or have you lost count?"

"You can't speak to me like that. I want to discuss—"

44

"You and I have nothing to discuss," Jessica interrupted fiercely. "I've got a plane to catch." She stalked away.

"Not any more," Margaret called after her. "Your flight home's been cancelled. You can ring the airline and check if you don't believe me."

"What? You can't do that!"

Diners stared as she stormed back, her fists clenched tightly.

"Sit down before you make me do something I won't regret." Margaret's tone was hard. Her hand slid beneath the table.

Jessica caught her breath. Was she armed? She wouldn't use a gun in a restaurant, would she? Jessica sank into a seat and took a sip of iced water; her throat was horribly dry. She hoped Margaret hadn't noticed her hand trembling. She wasn't afraid. Angry, yes. She wanted justice, but she'd settle for revenge if she had to.

"Good girl," Margaret said stiffly. "Now let's eat. I hope you're hungry. I'm told the lobster's out of this world." She snapped her fingers.

A waiter appeared, draped a starched linen napkin

over Jessica's bare legs and placed a large menu in front of her before moving on to the next table. She pushed the menu aside. "I'm not hungry. Why are you messing with me? You won, remember? I'm the idiot model who told a pack of lies. Everyone says so. Now why don't you back off and leave me and my family alone?"

"This is business. It isn't personal."

Hello? Margaret had undoubtedly leaked the stories to the press to damage her reputation in the modelling world. She'd also persuaded MI6 boss, Mrs T, to withdraw Jessica's invite to join Westwood – a division of the secret service that recruited models and other people from the fashion industry to work as undercover agents. Margaret wanted Jessica kept at arm's-length from MI6 in case they started listening to her accusations.

Jessica checked over her shoulder. "How can you say it's not personal when I've been out of work for most of the last six months and I lost my chance to join Westwood?"

Margaret stared back, expressionless. "It's hardly my fault you're not being booked for shoots, and I had nothing to do with the vetting for what you're referring to." She lowered her voice too. "However, I do know that MI6 is extremely careful about whom it recruits; it can't afford for models to crack up under the immense pressure of working for Her Majesty's Government."

"I don't believe a word you say. What do you want with me?"

She glanced across the table and noticed a third setting. Margaret was expecting someone else. Who else had she kidnapped and forced to come to lunch? The Mayor of New York? The President of the United States?

"How much do you know about Georgia?" Margaret said abruptly.

"What? The country?" That was the last question she'd expected. Was Margaret planning on giving her a geography lesson before she launched yet another attempt on her life?

"Yes, the country bordered on the north by Russia and on the south by Turkey and Armenia."

"Not much," Jessica admitted. "I remember it was on the news. Dad said it was fairly volatile some years back."

Margaret sipped her wine. "That's an understatement.

It's suffered bloody revolutions and wars throughout its history."

"And what does that have to do with me exactly?"

Margaret put the glass down and leant forward. "We have a contact – born in Georgia and now living in Russia – who needs MI6's help. *Your* help, to be precise."

Jessica snorted. "I'll pass, thanks. Helping you didn't work out so well for me last time, remember? My dad and I almost died thanks to you and your friend, Allegra Knight. And I don't even work for MI6."

Margaret settled back in her seat. "Yes, poor Jack. I'd heard he's ill. Is he still in hospital? A private hospital – one paid for by MI6 in lieu of his years of service?"

Margaret's words sliced through Jessica like a knife, but she couldn't risk showing any emotion. Things were really bad at home, Margaret must know that. While captive in Paris, Allegra had injected her dad with poison, which had badly affected his MS – a disease affecting nerves in the brain and spinal cord. Jessica had saved him, but his doctor didn't yet know his long-term prognosis. It didn't look good.

She thrust her chin in the air. "You know Dad's in a bad way. So do me a favour and drop the concerned act."

"It's such a tragedy." A smile hovered on Margaret's frosted pink lips. "I hope you have large family savings because apparently there's a problem with his medical bill. I'm told that MI6 has frozen payments to the hospital."

"No!" Jessica gasped before she could stop herself.

Her dad had needed specialist medical help immediately due to his condition; he couldn't wait weeks or even months for a referral to an NHS doctor. MI6 had pulled some strings and he was being seen by the world's top expert on MS. His treatment would run into tens of thousands of pounds; money they didn't have, especially now he was too ill to work. She used to help him out on cases, but she couldn't do surveillance and plant bugs all by herself, so they had been forced to turn down a string of clients over the last few months.

"People are questioning why we're paying for the treatment of an operative who left the service years ago," Margaret continued. "Of course, I can silence those questions and unfreeze the payment immediately if you agree to help me."

"So now you're blackmailing me, on top of everything else! Why am I not surprised?"

"This is a mutually beneficial situation. You help me in this small matter, and MI6 will continue to pay your father's hospital bills."

Jessica threw her napkin on the table. "How *do* you sleep at night?"

"Perfectly well, thank you. So will you help us, or are you going to start taking on catalogue work to scrape together the money for your father? After all, who knows what jobs you'll get after *this* shoot? Not everyone is as open-minded as Sebastian."

Margaret's threat was clear. She'd spread her poison around the fashion industry once more and make sure a photo shoot like today's never happened again.

"Do I have a choice?" Jessica snapped. "What is it you want me to do? I thought you told Mrs T that I was unsuitable for this work? I'm supposed to be unstable?"

"It's simple. We need you to protect this man's daughter for the next week."

She nodded towards a huge bulk of a man, wearing heavy gold rings and an expensively cut black suit. He powered through the restaurant, flanked by two equally large men in dark glasses. Jessica noted his drooping white moustache and eyes that were as dark and hard as granite. They darted around the room as if he were looking for someone. With a sharp nod of his head, the men beside him peeled off and stood at opposite walls, keeping guard. Their hands rested inside their jacket pockets. They were armed.

The man sat down at their table with his back to the wall and reached for the bread basket. He took two rolls, pulling off pieces and stuffing them into his mouth without acknowledging Margaret or Jessica.

"This is Levan Ingorokva," Margaret said pleasantly. "I think you know his daughter, Katyenka, already?"

"Kat the brat?" The words slipped out before she could stop them.

The oligarch chewed slowly, studying Jessica's horrified face. "She has been called a lot worse. Congratulations. You're her new bodyguard."

CHAPTER FOUR

"No way!"

Jessica would have to find another way of getting the money for her dad's treatment – like land a massive ad campaign, or donate a kidney, or win the lottery. Anything but *this*.

Mr Ingorokva shot a quizzical look at Margaret. "I thought you said she'd cooperate?" He cracked his knuckles one by one.

"We've discussed the private medical arrangement," Margaret said.

"Which is in addition to the expenses, paid for by myself" he added. "You won't be out of pocket, I assure you."

"She's reconsidering her options – aren't you, Jessica?"

She glared back at Margaret. Did she have a choice? But how could she explain in a diplomatic way to this man that his daughter was a monster?

"I think you should know I'm not Kat's best mate or anything, and I'm certainly not a professional bodyguard."

Mr Ingorokva shrugged. "I don't have time for personal feelings. This is a business arrangement. I want you to watch over Katyenka and never leave her side. It's as simple as that." He gestured for the waiter, before barking off his order: roast venison with sides of vegetables and fried potatoes.

Yeuch. Who'd want to eat that on such a scorching hot day?

"Why do you need me? She has bodyguards twice my size. They've followed her all around New York this week."

"You mean the ones that she gives the slip as easily as that?" Mr Ingorokva clicked his fingers. "Losing them has become a game to my daughter. But you could stick to Katyenka like glue. She'd never suspect a thing from a fellow model."

Jessica shuddered at the horrible thought. Kat

would probably have a more violent reaction if she ever found out what he was suggesting.

"I am not asking you to like her," he stressed. "Katyenka is spoilt, I admit, but she's all I have left. I will do anything to protect her."

"From what, exactly?" Jessica asked.

Mr Ingorokva exchanged looks with Margaret. "I've made some enemies over the years, and this has made Katyenka a possible target. I will not let history repeat itself."

"What do you mean? Has something happened before?"

Mr Ingorokva's face clouded over as he buttered a roll. He remained silent.

Margaret dodged answering her question too. "Mr Ingorokva has received numerous death threats against Kat. They have recently become more frequent. All refer to the coming week as Kat's last. We have every reason to believe the letters are genuine and could be acted upon imminently."

"Katyenka knows nothing of this," said Mr Ingorokva, fiercely, "and she'll never need to find out if you do your job properly."

"Did I hear right? You want me to be a human shield?" Jessica glared at the pair. "To risk my life for *her*? To take the bullet that's meant for Kat in return for my dad's medical bills being paid?"

"If that's what it takes," Mr Ingorokva growled.

"Brill!" Jessica exclaimed, slapping the table. "It's exactly the holiday job I always wanted. When can I start?"

Mr Ingorokva glowered at her.

"I understand your concerns, but it will never come to that," Margaret said. "You'll be an extra pair of eyes and ears on the ground for Mr Ingorokva, to help him feel more reassured. You'll be living on board his private yacht in Monaco and have backup from a team of armed bodyguards."

"It's the biggest in the world," said Mr Ingorokva, proudly.

"Great – so there'll be plenty of places for a potential killer to hide," Jessica retorted.

Mr Ingorokva muttered something in Russian, which obviously wasn't a compliment. Margaret replied, also in Russian. She gazed at Jessica.

"The yacht is subject to regular security sweeps,

courtesy of MI6," she said. "I've taken fingerprints and personally checked the credentials of everyone on board."

"Including myself and Katyenka," Mr Ingorokva snarled. "Was that really necessary?"

"Of course. It will help us eliminate suspects, should anything happen. I'm sure you'll agree it's in everyone's best interest that your business runs smoothly and without incident this week."

Mr Ingorokva gave a brusque nod and turned back to Jessica. "So what is your answer, Miss Cole?"

"Kat will never go for this. She's not exactly going to be delighted about me rocking up in Monaco."

"Leave my daughter to me," he said firmly. "She will do as she's told. I have already come up with a cover story. I'm sponsoring a gala ball in Monaco to raise money for Russian child cancer patients. A catwalk show will take place in the Grimaldi Palace. You and Kat will be the stars, and will feature in a pre-ball publicity shoot. Kat won't be able to resist the glitz and glamour. You see, I have thought of everything."

Yes, unfortunately, he had.

"Will you do this?" Mr Ingorokva asked.

Margaret's eyes bore into Jessica's. She had the feeling she was about to make the biggest mistake of her life.

"Yes." The word slipped out.

Mr Ingorokva grinned, revealing two gold teeth. He gave her a bone-crunching handshake before shoving his chair back. A waiter hovered nearby with his order, but he batted the roast venison away.

"I am meeting Katyenka now and will break the good news to her. A car will pick you up at six p.m. to take you to the airport. We fly to Monaco tonight. *Do svidaniya* – 'until our next meeting'."

He gave a small bow and stalked out, joined by his security guards. Jessica gazed across the table at Margaret.

"This should be a blast," she muttered. "So unfreeze my dad's payment right now, please."

"Once the job is completed, you have my word, the transaction will go ahead and will not be stopped again."

"Your word doesn't count for a great deal," Jessica said. "I want it in writing."

"That can be arranged. Any other demands?"

"How about a proper briefing? Why is someone trying to kill Kat? Do you have any suspects? What business deal is Mr Ingorokva involved in that MI6 wants to go smoothly? What did he mean about not letting history repeat itself?"

Margaret laughed but her eyes were glacial.

"I'm afraid this job works on a need-to-know basis," she said tightly. "Those questions are above your security clearance level. You've been told everything you need to complete this mission successfully. I'll be your point of contact on the ground in Monaco, giving you updates as and when necessary."

"So I'm basically being kept in the dark? When my life's being put at risk?"

"That's the nature of our job," Margaret replied. "The stakes are high, but the rewards will be huge if you are successful. You and your father won't have to worry about your hospital bill or even your mortgage debts. It'd be so sad if you lost your home. You grew up there with your mother, didn't you? There must be so many memories of Lily attached to the house."

Reeling, Jessica gripped the table. She couldn't bear hearing Margaret mention her mum's name. She'd always believed her death had been an accident; that she'd been killed in a helicopter crash when Jessica was four. But there was more to it than that. Her mum was a former model and ex-Westwood agent, like her grandmother Mattie before her. She'd been investigating the same terrorist, Vectra, when she died. It was possible he'd sabotaged the helicopter, with Margaret's help. But again, she had no proof.

"You don't get to talk about my mum."

"I'm just pointing out what you have to gain – and lose – from this mission. It'd be terribly sad if the bank foreclosed on your house."

Margaret was taunting her. She'd done a detailed background check on her dad to gain more leverage today. Margaret had guessed she could never risk losing their family home. She would have to take the job, however dangerous, to save it.

"Now it's my turn to set out demands," Margaret said. "There are certain conditions that I must insist upon."

"Such as?"

"Total secrecy. You can't breathe a word about this mission to anyone, including your father or grandma.

As far as your family is concerned, you're embarking on a week's holiday on a friend's yacht before taking up a lucrative modelling job in Monaco. It'll be booked through your agency, like any other job."

Jessica gaped at her. Margaret was deliberately cutting her off from her family. She knew that her dad and Mattie would never let her become a human shield; she didn't want to give them the opportunity to talk her out of such a dangerous job.

"What else?" Jessica steeled herself.

"You report to me and me alone."

She gave a curt nod. "I understand."

"Then everything's settled," Margaret said. "I expect daily updates in Monaco via a protected email account. The details will be sent to you before you leave tonight."

"Haven't you forgotten something? Isn't this the part where you give me some gadgets so I can protect myself in Monaco?"

Margaret's lips curled into a sly smile. "I'm afraid MI6 is experiencing a few cutbacks. I can't justify giving away expensive gadgets to a fourteen-year-old girl when they could help one of my agents in the field. I hope you understand. As I said before, this isn't personal."

Jessica felt an icy hand grip her heart. She understood all too well. She was being sent into a life-threatening situation, unarmed and without the support of her dad and Mattie. The job was a ruse.

Margaret didn't want her to make it back at all. She knew that someone would listen to Jessica's story about Paris eventually and couldn't afford to let that happen. This was her final stab at getting rid of her.

Margaret was sending her on a suicide mission.

"I know it's not great timing and I'm sorry," Jessica said for the millionth time. Back in the hotel room, she'd spent the last twenty minutes getting a strip torn off her by Mattie. Her grandma was seriously unimpressed that she'd missed her flight home and was heading to Monaco on a jolly instead.

"We'd all like a holiday, but some of us have to visit your father in hospital," Mattie persisted. "Or rather, we *want* to visit your father. He's still poorly, you know, and he's terribly cut up about Nathan. He hasn't got over what the doctors said."

Jessica flinched. She didn't want to go away but coming home right now wasn't an option. She couldn't tell Mattie what she was up to for fear of Margaret pulling the plug on her dad's expensive treatment and risking their house. She had to find a way to live long enough to fulfil the brief *and* expose Margaret.

"Look, I'll be back before you know it. I'll make it up to you both, I promise."

"Hmm." Mattie sounded unconvinced. "I thought you couldn't stand Katyenka, anyway."

"She's not *so* bad on a scale of one to ten."

"Well she's obviously more important than your father and I."

Her grandma had made her feel guilty enough. "The taxi's arrived to take me to the airport," she lied. "I'll ring you when I get to Monaco. Give Dad a big kiss from me. Bye!"

She cut Mattie off as a text arrived from Jamie after a million of hers. She'd left a long message on his voicemail, explaining how she'd be away for another week and was sorry.

: (

That was it? Jamie was so peeved he couldn't be

bothered to actually write a proper message. She added him to the list of people who were mad at her. Becky couldn't believe she was passing up the chance of going to Jamie's gig either.

R u mad? she'd texted back.

She must be. She'd allowed her worst enemy to talk her into a taking a job that could kill her.

The bedroom door banged open and Kat stormed in, accompanied by a hotel employee carrying dozens of designer bags and shoeboxes. Flinging a few dollars in his direction, she shooed him out. She turned towards Jessica, her face flushed scarlet.

"I don't know how you've managed to con Papa into believing we're friends," she fumed. "But I'm used to hangers-on trying to take advantage of me. I always manage to get rid of them, so don't get too comfortable on Papa's yacht. Your freebie won't last long."

"Fine by me. I'm as surprised as you that your dad press-ganged me into coming. He didn't take no for an answer, so I guess we both need to make the best of a bad lot."

Kat reddened. It hadn't crossed her mind that Jessica might be a reluctant guest.

"The Merc's waiting to take me to Papa's private jet at the airport," she snapped. "But you can take a cab."

"Fine." Jessica pulled her suitcase to the door and slammed it behind her.

Was there anyone left in the world who didn't hate her guts?

CHAPTER FIVE

Kat shoved her white, tasselled Gucci bag into a tray and stepped through the airport X-ray machine. An alarm sounded and a woman approached with a handheld scanner.

"Oh, please!" Kat rolled her eyes dramatically. "Don't you people ever remember? It's my platinum bracelet. It always sets the alarm off. You should know that by now. I travel through here often enough." Pouting, she folded her arms. "I don't see why I have to be checked at a private airstrip anyway."

"Because it's the law, ma'am," the woman replied. "Even for *VIP*s like yourself."

Jessica stifled a giggle, but Kat was oblivious to the sarcasm. The woman zapped her up and down with the scanner and allowed her through. Jessica was next. She'd emptied her pockets. She didn't have any nail files or scissors in her hand luggage, so she'd be OK. As her blue Mulberry handbag passed through the scanner, the man behind the computer stopped the conveyor belt and signalled to his colleague. They talked intensely for a few seconds. The woman who'd scanned Kat joined them.

"Is there a problem?" Jessica asked as the woman walked back, carrying the bag.

"You'll need to accompany me," she replied.

"What's she done now?" Kat taunted. "Is she carrying a bomb?"

"Ma'am, I seriously suggest you don't use that word again unless you want to stay the night in police cells," the woman shot back. "And you don't get VIP treatment there."

Kat scowled as Jessica was marched to a side door.

"There has to be a mistake," Jessica protested. "What did you find in my bag?"

"Go in." The woman held open the door and pushed her inside, passing her the handbag.

She jumped as the door clicked shut behind her. A

man in a grey suit stood with his back to her in the centre of a small, stuffy room. The strobe lighting blinked intermittently overhead, hurting her eyes.

"I don't know what this is all about. My bag doesn't—"

Her mouth fell open as the man turned around and pushed a pair of glasses up his nose. It couldn't be. It was *impossible*. An ugly red gash snaked through his closely shaven grey hair. She took in the glasses and bitten fingernails. His face was pale and considerably thinner, but it was definitely him.

"You're ... you're..." Her voice cracked.

Nathan Hall pushed his glasses up his nose. "Correct. I'm out of the coma."

Jessica ran towards him but stopped. She hadn't known he existed until six months ago. He'd fallen out with her dad after her mum's death, and hadn't been part of her life until Paris. Back then, she'd totally distrusted him. She'd accused him of being Starfish. If she remembered correctly, she'd also punched him in the face.

"Yeah, it still hurts," Nathan said, rubbing his jaw.

Yikes. Could he read minds?

"You've got a strong left hook." Nathan's eyes twinkled but he made no move to embrace her, even though they stood within touching distance.

"I d-d-don't understand," Jessica stuttered. "The hospital said there was no hope, that it'd be best if visitors stayed away. Dad—" Her eyes filled with tears as she stared at him. "Dad's been really cut up. I need to tell him the doctors got it wrong; you're OK."

Nathan grabbed her wrist as she rummaged in the handbag for her mobile. "I'm sorry but I can't let you do that. Jack mustn't know."

"What do you mean? My dad needs to be told right away. These last six months have been so hard on him. He knows he should never have accused you of being involved in mum's accident. He says he wasn't thinking right at the time and needed to blame someone. He wants to make things right with you; please give him the chance to do that."

Nathan let go of her wrist. He ran a hand through his crew cut, exposing the sharp contours of his skull. "The fewer people that realize I'm back, the better."

"No. You're wrong. You've no idea what's been going on. While you were in a coma, Margaret framed you. You have to clear your name."

"I do know. I remember..." His voice faltered. "I remember how *you* distrusted me."

"I'm sorry." Jessica swept her hair from her face. "Margaret convinced me you were Starfish, the way she did everyone else at MI6. When I realized the truth, only Dad and Mattie would listen."

"I don't blame you," he said softly. "I was tough on you in Paris." He placed a hand on her shoulder. His grip was gentler this time. "Unbelievably tough. But I assure you, not everyone at MI6 believes Margaret now."

Jessica's face brightened. "So arrest her! She's here in New York."

"I know. I had the same instinct when I woke up two months ago. Mrs T filled me in on what I've been accused of. She didn't believe me at first, but agreed to keep my recovery secret until she checked out my story."

Nathan paced up and down the room. His suit hung off his emaciated frame and his right hand shook slightly. Her dad would be shocked by the way he looked. Would they finally be able to put their differences aside and make up? She shook her head. All that family stuff was a distraction right now.

"Did Mrs T manage to connect Margaret to Allegra Knight and Vectra?"

"Not conclusively," Nathan said. "But she did link Margaret to an off-shore bank account that has been receiving regular, unexplained monthly payments for years. She also discovered suspicious activity on a computer at MI6 and a disposable phone Margaret is believed to have used. It was enough to make Mrs T doubt her, but not enough to secure a conviction."

Jessica's shoulders sagged. "So Margaret's going to get away with everything? Again?"

Nathan shook his head. "Not necessarily. That's why Margaret needs to think I'm still in a coma. Her guard is down. She'll slip up, and this time we'll catch her. That's the reason I'm here; Mrs T needs me to gather intelligence on her dealings with Mr Ingorokva. We don't believe they are completely above board."

He gestured for her to sit. Jessica slid into a plastic chair. She hadn't noticed until now how jelly-like her legs felt.

Nathan pushed his glasses up his nose again. "We're worried about Margaret's motives for getting you involved with Mr Ingorokva. Mrs T said it was Margaret's idea that you were approached to shadow Katyenka. There were other options, but she was adamant that it had to be you. Her refusal to consider using trained Westwood operatives raised Mrs T's suspicions too."

He leant forward in his chair. "We know how Margaret persuaded you to take the job. I've made sure your father's hospital bills have been processed so she can't blackmail you any more. It's up to you whether you want to go ahead with this mission. You could back out if you want. I'll do this alone."

"I want to help. We can get Margaret together."

"I hoped you'd say that." He reached down for his large brown leather briefcase and pulled out a file. Jessica stared at him, surprised. She wasn't used to this. Back in Paris, he'd ordered her to stay out of his investigations. Now, she was at the heart of them. Things *had* changed.

"Mr Ingorokva is a very useful asset to MI6, which is why this security brief was approved in the first place." He slowly flicked through the pages. "He has information we want."

"Such as?"

He looked up. "Details of Vectra's criminal network. Mr Ingorokva's worked with him in the past."

Jessica's eyes widened. "I thought he was dodgy but I didn't realize he was *that* dodgy."

"Mr Ingorokva made his fortune when the USSR collapsed, mainly through his engineering business and the oil and gas industries. Some of his deals were legitimate but many weren't. He survived a previous assassination attempt – a car bomb that killed his wife, Lilya, when Katyenka was a baby. However, the people behind that are serving life in prison in Russia. We don't believe there's any connection to these latest death threats."

Jessica gripped the table. Lilya. Lily. She and Kat had both been little when their mums were killed. It wasn't a pleasant bond. Nobody wanted murder in common.

"So he wants protection for Kat in return for providing info about Vectra?" Her voice cracked with emotion.

"In part. He also has contacts that could help us track Allegra Knight."

"No way!"

"Mr Ingorokva's very well connected. His information's already led MI6 to South America."

Nathan pulled out a grainy black-and-white photo and pushed it towards her. It showed a woman wearing a large summer hat.

"It could be anyone." She pushed the photo away.

"Except it's not. This picture was taken in Brazil six months ago, shortly after Allegra escaped from Paris. It's been run through facial-recognition technology. It works by matching a grab from CCTV footage to a faceprint in our watch-list database. It's definitely Allegra Knight, without a shadow of a doubt."

Jessica shuddered. "Where is she now?"

"That's what we'd like to find out. The trail went completely cold after South America, but we believe that Mr Ingorokva can help us trace her again. He's indicated that he will if this mission is successful."

"It doesn't make any sense," Jessica said, shaking her head. "Why would Margaret want *me* to get involved with Mr Ingorokva when he could lead

MI6 to Vectra and Allegra – two people who could incriminate her? She must realize there's a chance I might discover the connection."

"That's what we want to know. Margaret's taking a massive risk heading this mission, yet she pushed for this brief *and* to bring you along. We need to find out why."

"Whatever's happening, it's going down this week," Jessica said slowly. "Margaret mentioned that Mr Ingorokva has a business deal that MI6 wants to go smoothly. She wouldn't tell me what it was."

"That part's correct. The British Government has a vested interest in the current president of Georgia winning this week's election. If a militant opposition party takes power, terrorists will gain legitimacy. The region will be destabilized and there will be huge implications for neighbouring countries and even the UK. MI6 is charged with stopping that from happening."

"And how does Mr Ingorokva come into this?"

"A member of his network infiltrated the opposition party and discovered their plans to rig ballots," Nathan said. "For a price, Mr Ingorokva is arranging for the rigging to be blocked to ensure that the opposition party doesn't take power. The deal will be finalized in the next few days. Margaret is arranging the transfer of cash."

Jessica nibbled on a nail. "I don't get it. What will she get out of this deal?"

"On the surface, nothing. It's a routine job. But I suspect she's spotted an opportunity that isn't on our radar. Not yet, anyway."

"What can I do to help?"

"Keep an eye on Kat, as instructed, and find out why Margaret's so interested in Mr Ingorokva."

"That sounds easy enough."

"Nothing is ever easy in this business, or without danger. Remember that." Nathan checked his watch. "We need to press on. We don't have long before Mr Ingorokva will become suspicious." He pulled a pink make-up bag out of his case. "I'm sure you've already guessed. These aren't ordinary cosmetics."

Jessica's eyes gleamed. "Gadgets! So Margaret was lying when she said there wasn't enough money in MI6's budget to give me anything?"

"What do you think? Let's start with this." Nathan unzipped the bag and handed her a Chanel lipstick.

"Nice colour. It's the right shade of red." Jessica twisted the lipstick up. "But what does it do?"

"Turn the base a fraction of an inch anticlockwise and you'll hear a click."

Jessica obeyed. A tiny probe blinked.

"It's a movement sensor," he explained. "Keep it upright on a solid surface and it'll detect any movement, however small, within a three metre radius."

He dropped a pair of diamond earrings into the palm of her hand. "Wear these at night and they'll alert you if the sensor is activated."

"That could be useful," Jessica said, examining the jewels.

"So is understanding Russian. That's a must for this mission."

"Er, which I don't."

Nathan handed over a chrome iPod nano with earphones. "This works like any other iPod, so you can download your music as normal. However, flicking this switch at the bottom activates a microphone that will automatically translate any language into English. It has a ten metre radius."

"It's unbelievable!" Could she persuade Nathan to let her keep the iPod once this was all over? It'd come in handy in Spanish lessons.

"The diamond earrings do virtually the same by twisting the butterflies at the back, but they have a much smaller range; you'll need to be standing nearby for the instant language translator to work. Only use the earrings in a situation where it'd look odd to pull out your iPod and you're in close proximity to a target."

"OK. What's next?"

Nathan whipped out a pair of black Gucci sunglasses. "The best sunglasses you'll ever own."

Jessica raised an eyebrow. It was hard to beat her dad's thermal-imaging ones.

"Very stylish," she said, trying them on. "Kat will be jealous. They must cost a fortune."

"Even more now we've modified them. Press the tiny button on the right of the lens and you'll activate an enhanced-reality program linked to GPS. Buildings and roads will be named as you look at them and the program will calculate short cuts and escape routes. It's a bit like being in a video game."

OK, so this was *way* better than her dad's pair.

"They have built-in X-ray vision, which will help you scan for weapons," Nathan said. "You can also take photographs, check people against facial-recognition technology and criminal-records data, as well as search confidential MI6 files."

"Awesome!"

"Remember, only access files if you have to. It will automatically flag up a record of the activity at MI6. We don't want Margaret being tipped off about what you're up to."

Jessica nodded. The glasses were too cool for words. She wanted to try them out but Nathan had already moved on.

"This is a loose-powder compact. Blow it into the face of an attacker and it'll knock them out for at least ten minutes. It also causes temporary amnesia. The lid has X-ray vision."

Jessica examined the Swarovski-encrusted gold case. "I remember this." She'd been given something similar by MI6 before, but this one had loads more bling. Maybe she could use it on Kat when she was *really* annoying.

"It's got extra modifications now. Press the centre gemstone and it will scan, photograph and store fingerprints. It's also useful if you're on the move and need to photograph documents."

Nathan pulled out a plain silver pendant before she had time to play with the compact. "Put this on now and keep it on."

She carefully removed her mum's necklace and swept up her long, strawberry-blonde hair. Her throat felt bare without it. He fastened the clasp and helped do up a silver charm bracelet.

"What do you think?"

"Cool, I guess, but what can I do with them? Swing from buildings using a secret nanowire?"

"No. You'll need to use this for those sorts of acrobatics." He clamped a gold Rolex on her wrist. "A tensile wire, ten times stronger than steel, shoots out from the base and will attach to any surface. The watch also contains a laser that can cut through steel, and the face pulls off to provide a telescope. Like this."

He gave a quick demo.

"Cool. And the necklace? Don't forget that." She

touched the pendant. It was small but surprisingly heavy.

"Our gadgets team is particularly proud of this," he admitted. "Use it if you're deprived of oxygen either on the ground or underwater."

"How?"

"Bite the pendant hard and breathe in. It'll give you enough oxygen for approximately seven minutes."

Jessica examined the metal. Fingers crossed, she'd never need to use this. She put her mum's necklace in her pocket. She'd much prefer to wear *that* but it only had fond memories attached. It couldn't save her life like this pendant.

"The bracelet has a totally different function," Nathan continued. "It contains enough explosives in the heart charm to take down a three-storey building, so my team tells me. It's an early prototype and hasn't been used in the field before."

Eek. She undid the bracelet. She didn't fancy wearing explosives on a plane. What if it accidentally went off?

"What do you think's going to happen on this yacht?" Jessica gasped. "World War III?"

"We have no idea. That's why you need to be well-prepared. I wish I knew what Margaret had up her sleeve."

He ran through the real functions of a sequin Stella McCartney evening bag, a can of hairspray, a hairslide, face cream and nail polish. He placed a pair of trainers on the table.

"They're the right size. Pull the tag at the bottom and you can fire a taser."

"Will they give me supersonic speed as well?" Jessica said, trying them on.

"Sadly, no. But give it a few years and I'm sure our gadgets division will have cracked it." He checked his watch again. "You need to get going. Mr Ingorokva won't be able to hold his flight much longer."

Jessica removed her trainers and packed the gadgets into her handbag. "I still wish I could tell Dad you're OK."

"I promise we will when this is all over. In the meantime, be careful and don't trust anyone. I'm catching a flight to Monaco tonight and will be in contact when I arrive."

"OK. See you soon." Jessica hesitated again.

Shaking his hand was way too formal, but a hug seemed odd after talking about MI6 business. What should she do? Behave like his goddaughter or an agent? Nathan wasn't giving away any clues.

Jessica walked out, holding her handbag tightly.

Mr Ingorokva and Kat scowled darkly as she approached. Jessica's mind whirred as she picked the skin around her finger. What criminal activity was he involved in? Did he have another motive for wanting her to guard Kat? She couldn't let her face betray her emotions. Mr Ingorokva had to trust her.

"What was going on in there?" He jerked his head towards the door. "My BBJ3 is waiting on the runway. We'll miss our slot if we don't hurry."

"Yes, you took forever," Kat said sharply. "I told Papa we should go without you but he wouldn't listen." She glowered at Jessica. Her eyes widened as she spotted her Rolex. "Nice fake."

Jessica ignored her and turned to Mr Ingorokva.

"I'm sorry. My nail file triggered the alarm and they insisted on searching all my hand luggage and suitcase, which had already been taken to the hold. Let's just get on the plane. I can't wait to see it."

"It's an amazing piece of engineering – a custom-built Boeing Business Jet, with over one hundred square metres of luxurious accommodation," Mr Ingorokva enthused. "It cost me a small fortune but was worth every penny. Don't you think, Katyenka?"

Kat glared at him. "Are we going to discuss it all day or are we actually getting on board? I'm starving. I want my lunch."

Her dad sighed. "Your wish is my command. Follow me."

CHAPTER SIX

"Wow." Jessica's jaw dropped. Where were the cramped rows of seats with pull-down trays and overhead lockers? An expanse of plush cream leather chairs and sofas scattered with brown silk cushions and small dark oak tables stretched out in front of her. Oil paintings lined the walls and crystal lamps dripped from the ceiling. Were those seat-belt clasps actually made of gold? This was beyond wow. Or double wow. It was like being in a Bond film.

"It's not bad, I guess." Kat brushed past and curled up on a sofa. "But I told Papa he should have bought a Boeing 747-430. It's not as cramped as this."

Mr Ingorokva scowled. "This is better."

"Cramped?" Jessica exclaimed. "Have you ever flown economy?"

"What's that?" Kat said, frowning.

Jessica burst out laughing. "Somehow, I don't think you'll ever have to find out."

"Make yourself at home in my cramped jet, Jessica," Mr Ingorokva said. "I must have a few words with the pilot."

Great. She couldn't wait to explore. "So, can I have a tour, Kat?"

"Knock yourself out. I'm busy." She shoved in her iPhone earphones and music pulsated out while she flicked through a glossy magazine.

Jessica shrugged. Exploring alone was far better. She placed her bag and thermal-imaging sunglasses on another sofa, a little distance away from Kat. Her new MI6 sunglasses were safely tucked inside their designer case. She definitely didn't want Kat getting her hands on them.

"Oh, Jessica."

Kat pulled out an earphone as she walked away. Kesha pumped out again. "Yes?"

"Never mind. Nothing."

Didn't she listen to anything other than Kesha? Jessica headed up a floating spiral staircase into an impressive lobby. She peeked inside a boardroom. Was that a touch-screen table? Lights flickered on the glass. She wouldn't mind one of those. She walked further along the corridor to a large lounge area with a gigantic flat-screen TV on the wall. This had to be Mr Ingorokva's private quarters. It led into a luxurious bedroom with a king-size bed. Off that was an en-suite bathroom.

As she turned around, she spotted a piece of paper on the mahogany dresser. She picked it up. Cut out letters from a newspaper spelt out a message.

SAY GOODBYE TO YOUR DAUGHTER.
THIS WEEK SHE DIES

"What the hell are you doing in here?"

Jessica jumped, clutching the note. Mr Ingorokva stood in the doorway, his face white with rage. "Didn't Kat tell you? I don't allow anyone on to this level, including her."

Jessica grimaced. Kat had conveniently forgotten

to tell her that crucial snippet of information. She'd wanted her to get off on the wrong foot with her dad. How predictable.

"I'm sorry. I found this." Jessica handed him the note.

Mr Ingorokva studied the death threat before screwing it into a ball and tossing it across the cabin.

"Don't you think we should keep that as evidence? We could test it for fingerprints."

"It's a waste of time," he snarled. "Whoever's doing this always wears gloves."

"How many letters have you received?"

"Enough for me to be worried. But they have always come through the mail."

"So this is the first time a note's been hand delivered?"

Mr Ingorokva nodded, rubbing his temple. "They never dared do this before."

"You realize it has to be someone close to you? Someone you wouldn't suspect? It's probably an employee. They have access to you and to your jet. You need to look at everyone and ask Kat—"

"You're not to say a word to Katyenka."

"But—"

"It's not up for debate. She mustn't hear anything about this. Keep close to my daughter and do as you're told, there's a good girl."

He paused at the door and stared back. His gaze was hard and unflinching.

"I'll hold you personally responsible if anything happens to Katyenka. I'm not the kind of man you want to make an enemy of. I'm sure Margaret's told you that."

Jessica opened her mouth to protest but he'd already gone.

It was past midnight on the following day by the time they arrived at Monaco harbour; Kat had insisted the private jet was diverted to Paris so she could visit her favourite jewellers. *Lilya* loomed over all the other multi-million pound yachts; it was practically a floating island, and that was saying something considering the size of everything else moored in the harbour. Jessica was assigned her own personal valet who carried her bags aboard. She wondered if she'd ever be able to find her way around the maze of corridors below deck, even in daylight.

"This way!"

Mr Ingorokva marched ahead and she had to half walk, half run to keep up. He didn't notice as Kat peeled away to her suite without a word. *Goodnight to you too.* Kat and her dad obviously weren't big on exchanging pleasantries.

"I think you'll be comfortable here." He stopped and swiped open a door, passing the card to Jessica. "It's one of our best suites."

No doubt Kat had the most luxurious one, but second best was incredible too. The cream room was filled with dark walnut furniture and a king-size bed, covered with expensive-looking silk throws. Jessica caught a glimpse of an en suite through the door; a marble bath and gold fittings. She tried not to look too impressed. How could she forget Mr Ingorokva's earlier threat? She didn't want to find out what would happen to her if the culprit managed to get up close and personal with Kat. It wouldn't be pleasant, that's for sure.

"We have private chefs on call twenty-four hours a day. They'll whip up fresh lobster ravioli and a Belgian chocolate fondant for you at three a.m. if you want. They've worked in the best Michelin-starred restaurants around the world."

Jessica nodded, looking about. Jamie and Becky would die when she told them about this back home – if they were still talking to her.

"I also took the liberty of enlisting a stylist who's been shopping for you today. Clara made sure you have an outfit for every occasion." Mr Ingorokva opened a large walk-in wardrobe and pulled out a purple sequined dress.

Yikes. He was kidding, right? She wouldn't be caught dead in that. "Thanks, but I think I'm all set clothes-wise."

Mr Ingorokva's nose wrinkled as he stared at Jessica's jeans and cut-off Topshop t-shirt.

"While you're employed by me, you need to dress the part. People come to the harbour to see my yacht, and to catch a glimpse of myself and Katyenka. Paparazzi turn up with long lenses. I have an image to keep up and so do the people who work for me. Remember that, please, and dress accordingly."

Did he really just say that? She had to bite her lip to stop herself from laughing. "I hadn't realized, sorry.

I'll make sure I wear my high-street clothes safely away from public view."

Mr Ingorokva's eyes narrowed. He looked as though he were about to say something but stopped himself. He stalked out, slamming the door behind him.

Poor Kat. Jessica was actually starting to feel sorry for her. At least she could walk away at the end of this holiday from hell, but Kat had to live with him all the time.

Jessica flicked through the wardrobe. Armani, Dior, Burberry, Versace. Every single item, from jeans and t-shirts to cocktail dresses, had a designer label. She spotted a stunning Yves St Laurent silver couture evening-gown that was encrusted with crystals and lined with ostrich plumes. Ha ha. Maybe she should wear this to breakfast to annoy Mr Ingorokva. A white envelope was attached to the plastic covering. Ripping it open, she pulled out a receipt. Each outfit was itemized, totalling 200 thousand euros.

"No way!"

That kind of money would get the bank off her dad's back, like, forever. Clara had splurged Mr

91

Ingorokva's cash on designer gear without a clue whether Jessica would like it or not. She clearly didn't know she had strawberry-blonde hair. Or that she was only fourteen. Some of this stuff wouldn't look out of place on a fifty-year-old ambassador's wife. She examined a horrific gown with huge shoulder pads and a feather boa. *Fancy dress at Halloween, maybe, but not at any other time of the year.*

She slammed the wardrobe door shut. It was a pity Clara hadn't bought her a bulletproof vest. Now that might prove useful this week.

Jessica scrolled through Facebook and Twitter on her iPhone – everyone, as in absolutely everyone, had been at Jamie's gig. Except for her. Becky had uploaded tons of pics. It sucked that she'd missed it. Would Jamie ever forgive her? She'd try to make it up to him if he'd see her; if she ever made it back. They were big "ifs".

She froze as she noticed a photo of Jamie surrounded by a gaggle of stunning girls. He was grinning, arms flung around a redhead and a brunette. Her stomach lurched. Did he have groupies? Had something happened with one of them? Both girls were gorgeous. She flung the phone down on the bed. She couldn't bear to torture herself any more.

Would Becky tell her if Jamie had hooked up with someone else? She was usually surgically attached to her iPhone and texted constantly. Maybe that was why she'd gone so quiet. She didn't want to upset her by telling the truth.

You weren't there for him, she imagined Becky saying. *He's moved on.*

That wasn't true, was it? Clearly he'd been annoyed that she hadn't made the gig. Shaking the thought from her mind, Jessica refocused. Jamie might be the last of her worries this summer.

Kat's cabin was next door. What if an attacker got into Jessica's cabin by mistake, looking for Kat? She had to be prepared. Rummaging through her handbag, she pulled out the gadgets one by one. Where were her thermal-imaging sunglasses? *Dammit.* She must have left them on the plane. How annoying! They'd be useful for spotting intruders in the dark. She unscrewed the red lipstick and activated the motion sensor before fastening the diamond earrings.

She changed into the silk pyjamas that had been

laid out for her, and settled back on to the bed, which was covered in the finest Egyptian cotton sheets. She'd never been in such a large bed before.

So this was how billionaires lived.

Still, she'd much prefer to be at home with Jamie and her friends and family. That was something Kat and Mr Ingorokva's money couldn't buy.

Jessica's ear throbbed horribly as she woke up. She glanced at the clock. It was four-thirty a.m. For a moment, she couldn't remember where she was. Squinting in the dark, she saw portholes and it all came back to her.

She must have lain awkwardly on her earring. She fiddled with the butterfly. The stud vibrated beneath her fingertips. The movement sensor was activated. Someone was in the cabin.

She flew out of bed, instinctively grabbing for her thermal-imaging sunglasses. *Blast!* She'd forgotten she'd left them on the plane. Groping for the light, she flicked it on. The room was empty but her ear ached. There was only one place the intruder could be – the wardrobe. She snatched up her Swarovski compact and flicked open the lid. One puff of powder and they'd be knocked out instantly. She threw open the door, slashing at the clothes, then took a step back.

Nothing. The en suite was all clear too. A tiny *creak* made her spin around.

"Who's there?"

The room was totally empty, yet she didn't feel alone. She had a funny prickling sensation at the back of her neck. Was that the sound of someone else's heart beating loudly, or her own? The hairs on her arms bristled as something shifted in her peripheral vision.

She spun around again. This was beyond spooky. She could have sworn something moved. Someone was standing right behind her before flitting across the room. She ripped her earring out; it was too painful to keep in while it was vibrating like this.

BANG!

Jessica jumped. The cabin door swung open, slamming against the wall.

She'd locked it. She knew she had. She ran into the corridor. It was empty. She darted to the left and turned the corner. No one was in sight. She doubled back and headed past Kat's room. That corridor was empty too.

She followed it to the end and turned around. It was impossible. No one could disappear that fast.

She let herself in her cabin again and stopped. A message was scrawled on the mirror in her scarlet lipstick.

LEAVE OR DIE

CHAPTER
SEVEN

Jessica tore pieces off her fresh croissant and pushed them around her bone-china plate. Whoever left the death threat on the private jet was probably here. They'd been in her cabin last night and could still be on the yacht, plotting their next move. She'd become a target because she was close to Kat. When would they strike again? Today? Tomorrow?

"Not hungry?" Mr Ingorokva looked up from his plate of sausage and eggs.

Jessica jumped and shook her head.

"Head chef can whip up pancakes, egg-white omelette or eggs Benedict if you prefer," he persisted. "He can do anything you want. Did I mention the last restaurant he worked in had two Michelin stars?"

Yeah. At every opportunity.

"No, that's OK, thanks. I didn't sleep very well, that's all."

"I can replace your bed today or rearrange your suite if you prefer." Mr Ingorokva dipped bread into his runny yolk and shoved it into his mouth. "You can move to another cabin but it won't be as large."

Jessica hesitated. She glanced across the table. Kat was painting her nails Chanel Pirate scarlet and studiously ignoring her new tutor Darya, who was attempting to make conversation in Russian. The woman was in her sixties, with bright-red unbrushed hair, a furrowed forehead and slender white fingers that were perfectly manicured. Clearly she paid more attention to her nails than the rest of her appearance. She wasn't wearing a scrap of make-up.

Jessica looked back at Mr Ingorokva. Didn't Kat have a right to know that something was *very* wrong on board? Her life was in danger, yet she was completely oblivious.

"Someone was in my cabin last night."

Mr Ingorokva shot her a daggers look.

"What?" Kat looked up, batting away her breakfast companion.

"Did you lock your door?" Mr Ingorokva dabbed his moustache with a white linen napkin.

"Yes, but—"

Mr Ingorokva glared at her. "Then it's impossible. I have state-of-the-art on-board security which would have detected an intruder. You must have been dreaming."

"Sometimes I dream that—"

"Not now, Katyenka."

Kat flinched. Jessica noticed her hand shook slightly as she returned to painting her nails.

Mr Ingorokva glanced at a bodyguard. "Review the security footage from last night. I want a full briefing in an hour."

The man peeled away and walked briskly out. Mr Ingorokva turned to Jessica.

"I will investigate this thoroughly but I know you're wrong."

"If you say so."

She met his gaze. Kat might be too afraid to stand up to him, but she wasn't. Someone had written on her mirror last night and it wasn't a ghost.

He shoved his plate back abruptly.

"Katyenka, take Jessica and Darya on a tour of the yacht this morning. I'll be busy all day and cannot be disturbed."

"But I wanted us to have lunch together. I have so much to tell you."

"Sadly, that's impossible. I have important business that can't wait. I'll have very little time for you or anybody else this week, so you'll need to keep your guest entertained."

Kat's bottom lip quivered. "But Papa!"

"Enough!" Mr Ingorokva banged his fist down, making everyone at the table jump. "I will have obedience! I will have respect! You are embarrassing me."

Kat burst into tears. Her tutor handed her a tissue and looked away, unwilling to get involved. She'd caught on to Mr Ingorokva's rules fast – do as you're told and keep your head down.

"It's OK, Kat. We'll find some fun things to do together." Jessica smiled at her. She never thought she'd find herself saying that.

Kat dabbed her eyes.

"Don't cry." Mr Ingorokva's face softened. He reached over and ruffled her hair. "You don't understand the pressures I am under, and nor should you. You're but a child, my *kotik* – my little cat."

He clicked his fingers and a bodyguard stepped forward, passing him a box. It was wrapped in silver tissue paper and tied with a large white bow.

Mr Ingorokva beamed. "This is for you, my dearest."

Kat managed a watery smile as she took the box.

"It's a Fabergé egg," he said, before she'd had chance to unwrap it. "It's the missing 1903 Royal Danish Egg, to be precise. My people have been looking for it for years and traced it to a private collection in Dubai. I made the owner an offer he couldn't possibly refuse."

"It's beautiful," Kat gasped.

She pulled out a light blue-and-white enamel egg that was ornately decorated with gold and diamonds. It was held up from a gold stand by lions and topped by an elephant, bearing a crown.

"An elephant! I adore elephants!" Kat clutched it to her chest.

"That's why I searched high and low for it. I only want the best for my *kotik*."

Jessica pushed back her plate. Honestly, if his peacock-like chest puffed up any bigger, he'd explode.

Kat raced around the table and threw her arms around him. "I love it, Papa. It's the best present, ever."

"Twenty million dollars is a small price to pay for your happiness."

Jessica raised an eyebrow. He had to bring that up, of course. Everything had a price tag where he was concerned, even his daughter's happiness.

"You must look after this egg, Katyenka," he said sternly. "You can't lose it like that Cartier bracelet. This is far more valuable. It will be kept in the safe in my study at all times."

"But I won't be able to look at it!" Kat protested. "Please, Papa. Let me keep it for one night. I shall go to sleep looking at it and thinking of you."

Mr Ingorokva hesitated. "Very well. One night then it must be locked away."

"Of course, Papa. Whatever you say."

"Good girl. Now I must go." He rose to his feet. "Darya will accompany you both to the Monte Carlo

Bay Hotel for a fitting after the tour and we will meet again for dinner at seven p.m. sharp. Good day to you all."

He stalked out, flanked by three security guards.

"Look what I got!" Kat dangled the egg in front of Jessica. "Are you jealous?"

She shook her head. She wouldn't trade lives with Kat for any amount of money.

"*Lilya* is over six hundred feet long – it's the biggest in the world." Kat rolled her eyes and inspected her glossy red nails.

She'd clearly given this tour many times before and didn't relish repeating it for Jessica and Darya.

"It has three swimming pools, two helipads and a crew of a hundred and fifty. It cost over 645 million dollars."

"How much?" Jessica blurted out.

"Are you deaf or what?" Kat snapped.

She didn't bother retaliating. It wasn't worth the fight. Kat's excitement at receiving a Fabergé egg had worn off and she was back to being her usual stroppy self.

Darya muttered something in Russian and Kat barked back. She repeated herself in English. "She wanted to know why the yacht's called *Lilya*. I told her to stop asking stupid questions."

Darya looked from one to the other, puzzled.

"It seems a reasonable question to ask," Jessica pointed out.

Kat hesitated. "If you must know, it's named after my late mother."

Jessica glanced away. She had to pretend she didn't already know. "I'm sorry."

Kat swept her long black mane away from her face. "Don't be. I was a baby when mama died. I don't remember anything about her."

"I was four when I lost mine, so I can remember some stuff. I think about her all the time. She was called Lily."

Kat looked startled. "Oh."

"So I guess we do have something in common."

"No we don't," she spat back.

Kat turned to Darya, who had moved closer. "Get out of my personal space, will you? You're like my shadow."

The woman looked puzzled until Kat repeated herself in Russian. She took a step backwards.

"The woman's an imbecile," Kat said, laughing. "And she dresses like a man!"

"Kat!"

Kat looked Darya up and down. Her eyes rested on the dark roots showing through her tutor's red hair. "She's got the worst dye job I've ever seen in my life."

"Ssshh."

"She doesn't speak a word of English, so you can say whatever you want. Papa employed her so we can talk in Russian all the time. He doesn't want me to forget the language. As if! He must be paying her by the word because she doesn't shut up."

She smiled brightly at Darya. "You're doing my head in and I'm going to get rid of you. Papa's appointments never last long. I make sure of that."

Darya grinned and nodded.

"Can we get on with the tour?" Jessica said, sighing.

"Of course. The sooner I finish, the quicker I'll be rid of you both." Kat flounced off, with a *clickety-click* of her tan Chanel sandals.

*

The yacht was unbelievable. It had taken two hours to explore a few of the decks above the waterline and they still weren't done. Jessica had counted twenty bathrooms, eight dining rooms, five bars, two cinemas and three libraries so far.

Next on the tour was the well-being area, which had its own swimming pool with a wave machine, a beauty salon, massage and treatment rooms, three whirlpool baths, a sauna and steam room. The area was surrounded by large golden statues of dolphins and crabs. They were hideous. Mr Ingorokva might have money but he sure didn't have taste.

"You can have a beauty treatment later if you want," Kat said, begrudgingly.

Jessica waited for her to add "because you need it", but she had to be flagging because she'd run out of insults.

Next to the well-being area was a sign saying "medical centre". Darya made a quiet remark to Kat.

"Yes, we do need to go inside," Kat said, repeating herself in English. "Papa asked me to show you everything. So here goes."

She flung the door open and smiled dazzlingly.

"Miss Ingorokva. To what do I owe this pleasure?" A handsome, dark-haired man stood up at his desk and strode towards them. He seized Kat's hand and kissed it. "I hope you're not ill?" The skin around his deep blue eyes crinkled with worry.

"I'm fine," Kat batted her eyelashes as she twisted a strand of hair around her fingers. "This is a tour for our new guests."

"Of course." He smiled warmly at Jessica and Darya. "Welcome. I'm Dr Andrei Fedorovna, Mr Ingorokva's new medical director."

"Well, new*ish*," Kat added. "Papa employed him months back."

Jessica guessed he was about thirty – twice Kat's age, but that didn't seem to put her off. Kat couldn't keep her eyes off him. Did he realize how much she fancied him? It was hard to miss. Kat wasn't exactly subtle, swishing her hair from side to side and hanging on his every word.

"Guests and crew members can make appointments to see me for medical problems, as well as physiotherapy and acupuncture," he said. "We also have a small operating theatre."

"You do operations on board?" Jessica asked.

"Only in an emergency – if we were out at sea and couldn't get back to land in time. But hopefully that won't happen. It's been routine stuff since I joined – ingrowing toenails and such like."

"Eeugh!" Jessica laughed. "Very glamorous!"

"I know! I get all the best jobs."

Kat's eyes narrowed. She slunk in front of Jessica, catlike, and flashed her perfect white teeth at Dr Fedorovna.

"I'll swing by later, Andrei," she purred. "I need to talk to you about something. Well, you know, something *personal*."

Dr Fedorovna reddened. "Of course. Please book an appointment through my secretary. You understand the procedure."

Kat flinched slightly.

So he *did* realize that Kat fancied him and was politely trying to give her the brush off. She probably spent an awful lot of time down here, pestering him.

"Good day to you all." Dr Fedorovna held the door open. Kat took one last longing look and left.

The decks below water level were just as impressive; a garage large enough for thirty luxury cars and an underwater viewing deck. But Kat had lost what little interest she had. She'd shoved in her earphones to block out Darya's chatting and was still sulking after the doctor's brush-off.

"That's it for the tour," she said, talking above the music. "I'm done."

"What about through there?" Jessica nodded towards a sealed door, guarded by three cameras and a control pad.

Kat sighed and removed her earphones. "That's Papa's security base. It's a restricted area."

"Why? What's inside?"

"Oh, the usual – a mini submarine and anti-aircraft missile system."

"Yeah, because that's usual," Jessica said, laughing.

Kat scowled back.

"Why does your dad need all that kind of stuff anyway?"

"Papa has lots of enemies. People are jealous of his wealth and power so he has to protect us. All the cabins are armour-plated, the glass is bulletproof and the security cameras use facial-recognition software to identify everyone on board and monitor their movements."

"Wow!" That was slightly reassuring.

"It's what you'd expect for a man in Papa's position. Both of us could be targeted because of his money and business dealings. That's why we've got so many bodyguards."

Kat sounded matter-of-fact. Why did her dad think she couldn't cope with hearing about the death threats?

"Let's go," Kat said flatly.

Jessica turned to follow but Darya was rooted to the spot, staring at the entrance to the security base. Kat barked at her in Russian. She jumped and brushed past Jessica, her face expressionless.

CHAPTER EIGHT

Tourists stopped and stared as Jessica and Kat arrived at the Monte Carlo Bay Hotel in a convoy of armour-plated cars, accompanied by nine bodyguards. If Jessica hadn't known better, she'd have said it was over the top. But maybe Mr Ingorokva *had* discovered something on the security footage from last night. He certainly wasn't taking any chances. Kat and Jessica had four guards each, with one trailing after Darya.

Kat tugged at her white Calvin Klein miniskirt as she pulled open the door to a large banqueting suite. Half a dozen models were draped about the room, chatting and flicking through magazines as they waited for the fittings to begin. Stylists steamed dresses and sorted through boxes of accessories. Jessica caught a glimpse of a long white Grecian gown as a stylist carefully unzipped it from its plastic case. Kat would nab that, no doubt. It was totally stunning. Everyone looked up briefly as Kat tottered in on silver Vivienne Westwood skyscraper sandals. She was heavily made-up with false eyelashes, shimmery blue eyeshadow and glossy, scarlet lips.

"I knew I should have worn something else," she whispered fiercely, eyeing up a stunning blonde model. The girl was make-up free, dressed simply in white jeans and a grey off-the-shoulder top.

Kat pulled bad-temperedly at her miniskirt again. "The fitting will have to be postponed. I'm going back to the yacht to change. My hair's not right either. It's all messed up."

She pulled out a diamond-encrusted compact from her cream Victoria Beckham handbag and used it to examine her porcelain complexion.

"This eyeliner's too blue. I don't know what Clara was thinking, buying it for me. She's hopeless. I might tell Papa to fire her."

"You look fine," Jessica reassured. "Stop worrying."

"Someone like you could never understand." She

112

recoiled as Darya placed a hand on her arm and pushed her roughly aside.

"Back off, why don't you? And I don't know what you lot are looking at either!"

The models glanced away as the stylists talked quietly.

"Calm down," Jessica said, steering Kat away. "You can't act like this. You should apologize to Darya."

"No way! I can't stand her. She'll be gone before the end of the week anyway."

Jessica glanced over her shoulder. Darya was slumped in a chair, dabbing her eyes with a tissue. Kat was right; Darya would be gone soon, but she would probably quit before Kat had her fired, and who could blame her when she was being treated so badly? She couldn't possibly be getting paid enough to put up with Kat's bad temper.

"What's got into you?" Jessica said. "You're acting like a first-class brat. Even more so than usual."

Kat flinched.

"Nothing," she said surlily. "I hate being watched like this all the time." She nodded at the bodyguards lining the room. "I don't know why Papa has to

113

employ so many. It makes me feel..." Her voice wavered as she glanced at the other models.

"Different. I feel different." Her eyes welled up.

"You like being different. You don't attempt to fit in."

Kat shrugged. "Sometimes I wonder what it would be like if I tried, you know, to fit in."

Jessica stared at her, surprised. It was the first time she'd seen her let her guard down. "You know, maybe—"

"Oh, forget it!" Kat's tone was hard again, as if she were annoyed at herself for being so honest. She flicked her hair over her shoulders, gave the blonde model a filthy look and sashayed over to the stylists. "Show me what you've got planned for the show. If I don't like it, you're all fired!"

Kat had first dibs on all the clothes, of course, but Jessica was thrilled with her line-up. So far she'd been fitted for a black-and-white corseted Vivienne Westwood full-length gown and two gorgeous lace dresses from Dolce & Gabbana – one red, encrusted with jewels, and the other gold and black with a huge, heavy medallion belt. She still had amazing dresses from Dior and Armani Privé to try on.

Kat had ignored the stylist's advice and opted for expensive, flashy designs that didn't actually suit her, but she wasn't in the mood to be argued with. One stylist had already fled the room in tears, and another had quit after Kat had roasted her for *almost* pricking her with a pin.

They'd only managed to fit in one quick run-through when Kat declared she was faint with hunger. Waiters wheeled in trolleys laden with smoked salmon, huge king prawns, a selection of meats and cheeses, salads, baskets of bread, pastries and fruit. Another trolley contained jugs of water and freshly squeezed orange juice.

Kat rolled her eyes and grabbed the sleeve of a passing waiter. "I can't eat any of this. Get me an egg white omelette with chives, a side salad – no dressing – and a glass of still mineral water at room temperature with an extra glass of ice on the side. I can't possibly drink tap water from a jug like that."

"Have you ever tried saying please?" Jessica asked as the waiter departed. So much for her wanting to be like everyone else.

She spat back some kind of insult in Russian, her mood darkening by the minute. What was wrong with her? She was being even more vile than usual.

Another waiter returned a few minutes later with a tray. Kat clicked her fingers. "You took your time. Over here."

She gestured for him to put her tray down on the opposite side of the room, away from everyone else, then sat with her back turned, picking at her omelette. She might as well put a sign on her back saying "go away". It was hard to work her out. Which was the real Kat? – the vulnerable one who allegedly wanted to fit in, or the prima donna who kept driving everyone away?

Suddenly, Kat looked over her shoulder, slammed down her knife and fork and stood up, clutching her glass of water. "What the hell are you doing?"

A stylist paused, scissors in hand as she unpicked a gown's hem.

"This hem needs altering."

"Leave it alone!" Kat said, glowering. "It's perfect as it is." As she stalked towards her, her foot caught in the handle of her handbag. She tripped, dropping the glass. There was a hissing noise and curls of smoke rose from the wet patch. An acrid smell filled the air.

"Aaaaagh!" Kat let out a blood-curdling scream. "Help me!" Doubled over with pain, she clutched her hand and fell to the carpet.

Jessica ran over and grabbed Kat's hand. An angry red sore festered at the base of her thumb. The wound deepened by the second, like something was burning into the flesh.

"It's killing me," Kat screamed. "Do something!"

Jessica snatched a jug of water from the trolley across the room and returned, dunking her hand into it. "Keep it in here."

She glanced over her shoulder at the bodyguards, who were talking into their mics as Darya hovered nearby, babbling hysterically.

"She needs to get to hospital right now!" Jessica shouted.

"An ambulance is on its way," a bodyguard called back.

Jessica held Kat's hand firmly in the water as tears rolled down her face. It looked like a serious burn, and this was the only way she knew how to treat one. But how had Kat hurt herself?

"What's going on? What is that?" Kat sobbed as she stared down at the red carpet. A hole had appeared, exposing the floorboards. The wood was being eaten away.

Frowning, Jessica examined the carpet. She pulled a comb out her pocket and prodded the liquid. The plastic immediately disintegrated.

"It looks like some kind of acid. I've seen sulphuric acid used in chemistry class and it acts really fast. It's colourless and eats through virtually anything."

Kat stared at the hole in the carpet. "Why was acid in my glass?"

Jessica squeezed her shoulder. This was a deliberate attempt on Kat's life, but she couldn't tell her that.

"Maybe it got mixed up in the kitchens. Someone could have been using it to clean the drains and left the bottle out. The waiter could have picked it up by mistake."

"Ohmigod, ohmigod. I could have been killed." Kat rocked back and forth as she nursed her hand.

"You didn't drink it, that's the main thing. It was

lucky you tripped." She glanced back at the handbag. "That saved your life."

"I was meant to drink it," Kat whispered, tears rolling down her cheeks. "Someone's trying to kill me, I know it. This isn't the first time they've tried."

"What do you mean?" Had she found out about the death threats? Kat had looked particularly interested when she'd told Mr Ingorokva that someone had been in her cabin last night.

Kat turned her anger to the approaching bodyguards before Jessica could quiz her further. "A lot of good you lot are! Wait until Papa finds out what happened. You'll all be fired!" She pulled Jessica towards her. "Tell Papa I need him right now. He must come to the hospital straight away."

"Of course."

The guards helped Kat to her feet.

"Come on," one barked. "We need to get you clear of the area."

Jessica stepped forward but a guard got in her way. His left hand remained tucked inside his jacket, holding a concealed weapon. "The ambulance is here. A car will take you back to the yacht."

"No! I'm going with Kat. It's what Mr Ingorokva would want. Check with him if you don't believe me."

"Fine," the bodyguard growled. "We leave right now."

"Mr Ingorokva wants updates every five minutes," another bodyguard muttered as they headed to the door.

"So Papa knows already? Is he meeting us at the hospital? What did he say about me exactly?" Kat was still firing questions as she was marched out.

Jessica grabbed Kat's handbag from the floor, ice cubes crunching beneath her feet. As she ran after them, she noticed a stick of eyeliner poking through a small hole in the bottom of the bag. The cream leather around it was discoloured. The acid must have splashed it too.

"How could you let this happen?" Mr Ingorokva shoved his face close to Jessica's. A bubble of spit burst on his lip as he yelled at her in his office on board *Lilya*. "This kind of security lapse is totally unacceptable. My daughter could have been killed."

"This isn't my fault," Jessica hit back.

She couldn't believe she'd had to leave Kat at the hospital to receive a face-to-face rollicking from Mr Ingorokva. He'd been too tied up with business to visit his only daughter, but he wasn't too busy to lay into her. The showdown was brutal and had lasted several minutes already.

Mr Ingorokva clenched his fists. "That's exactly what my daughter's bodyguards said right before I fired them all. They were lucky that's all I did to them."

Jessica glared at him. She refused to take a step back. "What about you? Is your conscience clear?"

"What do you mean?" Mr Ingorokva's nostrils flared.

"Did you get your bodyguards to give the hotel a once-over before we arrived? What are you actually employing them to do?"

Mr Ingorokva scowled back.

"I told you there was someone in my cabin last night, but you didn't warn Kat about the note on the jet," she continued. "If we had, maybe she wouldn't even have gone to the hotel today. She might have wanted to postpone the fitting."

"There was no intruder," he snarled.

Jessica planted her hands on her hips. "I didn't tell you everything in front of Kat this morning. Someone got into my cabin and wrote 'Leave or Die' on my mirror in lipstick."

Mr Ingorokva caught his breath as Jessica showed him a photo of the threat she'd taken on her mobile.

"I've already checked the footage," he said finally. "There's a camera just along the corridor from your cabin. No one entered your room all night. Except—"

"What?"

"Your cabin door swung open and shut at 4.30 a.m. and again at 4.34 a.m., but there was no one there. The camera doesn't lie."

"How is that even possible?" Jessica said. "My door was locked from the inside."

"I don't know. It could only be done using a master key card that I keep in this room. I've checked – it's still in the drawer. I'm getting my engineer to examine all the locks on board to make sure they're not malfunctioning."

"And if they're not?"

"Then I don't know how to protect my daughter from a ghost."

"Ghosts don't exist, Mr Ingorokva."

"So they say," he said tartly. "But I'm running out of explanations. Except for..."

"What?"

He shook his head. "Never mind."

Jessica shoved her hair behind her ears. This was the third time she'd heard a ghost mentioned in the last few days – first at the Grammys and then at the Frick Collection in New York. She couldn't think of a rational account for any of this either, but would never admit that to Mr Ingorokva.

"I need to check every employee who works on this ship and find out who holds a grudge against you," she said.

"Don't you think I've done that already? I've vetted everyone rigorously. All my employees have allegiances to my family, going back to my father's day. They can all be trusted."

"Then give *me* a list of your employees to check."

"Why? How will that help?" Mr Ingorokva looked puzzled.

"I can look at it with fresh eyes." With the help of her super-high-tech spy glasses, she'd be able to cross-check each employee against the MI6 database. That could turn up something useful.

"You think a slip of a girl can track down the culprit when my security brief couldn't?"

"That's why I'm here, isn't it? I can run anything I find past Margaret at MI6. She's the best, you know."

Would he fall for her lie?

Mr Ingorokva sniffed. "Margaret's already done her own security checks, but if you want to waste your time doing them again, be my guest. Anything else?"

"I'll ask Margaret to check the backgrounds of everyone at the casting and the kitchen staff and waiters who prepared Kat's tray. Maybe someone took a bribe to swap the water with acid. We should also get a forensic test of the carpet and Kat's bag to find out what kind of acid was used."

"It hit Katyenka's bag too?"

"Yes, but luckily she tripped over it and fell before she could drink from the glass."

"My poor *kotik*." Mr Ingorokva sat down heavily behind his desk. "She could have been killed."

"She's OK," Jessica said gently. "A tiny drop splashed her hand. The doctor doesn't think she'll be scarred permanently, but he referred her to a cosmetic surgeon for a second opinion."

"She'd better not be scarred," Mr Ingorokva said, pulling open his desk drawer. A black revolver lay on top of a sheath of paper. "Family honour is very important to me. I will take revenge on whoever's doing this to me."

"Don't you mean whoever's doing this to your daughter?"

Mr Ingorokva flicked on his computer, ignoring her.

"Kat needs you," Jessica said quietly. "You should be with her at the hospital. You're her dad. She doesn't have anyone else."

Mr Ingorokva slammed a file down on the desk. "How dare you tell me what I should and shouldn't be doing? Take this and get out of here now!" His other hand hovered near the revolver. His threat was clear.

Jessica grabbed the file and ran out, colliding with someone. "Hi!"

Kat smiled wanly, her arm in a sling. Her dark hair hung limply around her pale face and she looked like she'd been crying. Had she been eavesdropping all this time? If so, she'd realized that her dad cared more for his reputation than her.

"I had no idea you were back. Are you OK?" She touched Kat's arm, but she moved away.

"I guess. The hospital discharged me with painkillers and said to come back in a few days to meet with the cosmetic surgeon. I want to see Papa. He said to find him when I got out."

"He's in there," Jessica said, nodding at the door. "He'll be thrilled to see you."

She hoped for her sake he'd look up from his computer.

Kat stared at the file in her hand. "What did Papa want to talk to you about?"

"He wanted to know what happened, of course. He's worried sick about you."

"Really?" Kat brightened up.

"Of course he is," Jessica said, frowning. "He's beside himself."

"Cool. I can't wait to fill him in on all the details."

"Er, OK. I'll leave you to it. Your dad wanted me to pass this to his new security team." She brandished the folder. "I'd better go."

Kat knocked timidly at the door and let herself in. Jessica watched as Mr Ingorokva wrapped her in a bear hug. Kat kicked the door shut as they sobbed in each other's arms.

They were the most dysfunctional family she'd ever met.

CHAPTER
NINE

Nathan had been spot on about Mr Ingorokva. He *was* dodgy. Jessica had spent hours traipsing around the yacht, photographing crew members with her MI6 sunglasses and emailing the info to Nathan, as he'd requested. So far he'd reported back that thirty of them had criminal records, ranging from handling stolen goods to manslaughter – and he'd only vetted one fifth of the crew. One had served time for killing a business partner and most had links to the Russian mafia. Even the captain had been jailed for false accounting, and the beautician for money laundering.

Mr Ingorokva said he'd rigorously checked everyone's backgrounds, so he must be deliberately surrounding himself with criminals. It was going to make it a lot harder to whittle down a list of potential suspects when no one was squeaky clean.

But which one wanted to harm Kat, and why?

Jessica shivered as she remembered the revolver in Mr Ingorokva's study. How many times had he pulled the trigger? Someone who did business with a terrorist like Vectra and had links to Allegra Knight would go to great lengths to ensure his own survival. He must have a long list of enemies.

Perched on the side of her bed, she scanned the personnel list. It was going to take longer than she'd thought to find and photograph all of the crew. It was hard on a vessel this size; employees were scattered all over the place and had shift changes. Her heart skipped a beat as her phone rang. For a split second she thought it could be Jamie, but her dad's name flashed up. She pressed divert. She couldn't face lying to him about what she was up to. What if he mentioned Nathan's diagnosis again? She couldn't tell him that he was out of hospital and hiding out somewhere in Monaco, running checks on Mr Ingorokva's crew via a protected MI6 laptop. Jessica texted him instead, asking how he was and telling him that she was enjoying her holiday. She'd speak to him later. *Much* later.

Buzz! A text came back after a couple of minutes.

Stop avoiding your father and call him. He's worried about you. P.S. I know you're up to something. Your loving grandma.

Aaagh. Mattie never called herself "grandma" or let anyone else call her that either. It was her code for telling Jessica she was in *big* trouble. She had some kind of sixth sense for when Jessica was doing something she wouldn't approve of.

Have no idea what you mean. Great hols. Speak soon. Your loving granddaughter.

She'd only be able to hold off Mattie for so long. She was like a bloodhound when she picked up the scent of something suspicious, which wasn't surprising given her Westwood background.

Next, Jessica trawled back through the emails on her iPad. She'd already filed a report about the attempt on Kat's life to Nathan, as well as sending one to Margaret via a separate MI6 account. There was nothing new from Margaret – she'd already made clear in her last correspondence that the crew had been rigorously vetted by MI6 and that she should focus on the hotel staff. Hopefully, Margaret hadn't noticed the checks Nathan was doing.

Jessica scanned some newspaper cuttings Nathan had sent her earlier; useful background info on the current elections in Georgia and the president's battle against corruption. Share prices in the country were fluctuating amid uncertainty over the election's outcome, and demonstrations organized by the opposition party had broken out. Riots were feared over the next few days.

Work done, she lay back on her bed. She'd managed to duck out of dinner by faking a headache. She couldn't face another meal of tense silences from Kat and volcanic eruptions from Mr Ingorokva. She couldn't be bothered to get dressed up in her new designer gear either. Far better to slob out in her cabin wearing shorts and a t-shirt, and tuck into a tuna pasta salad, courtesy of the Michelin-starred room service. She called Becky while she waited.

"Hi! It's me!"

"Who?" Becky's voice sounded distant.

"It's Jessica!"

"I can't hear you very well. I'm on the Underground. Can we speak later? About to go into a tunnel."

"Sure," Jessica said. "But we haven't spoken in ages and I wanted to check—"

The phone went dead. She tried ringing Jamie next but his phone diverted to voicemail. She didn't bother leaving a message. What was the point? Neither of them seemed to want anything to do with her.

Her personal life was dead.

Buzz! Another text message landed as room service arrived.

Meet me in ten minutes at Sass Cafe.

Great. Now she had to ditch dinner even though she was starving. She wasn't sure if the text was from Margaret or Nathan, as the number was protected. Neither had mentioned meeting up in their earlier emails and she could hardly ring up Margaret and ask if it were her. Nathan had said he was picking up a new disposable phone in Monaco, so it *could* be him. Jessica quickly emailed him and waited for a reply. Nothing. She'd just have to turn up and find out who urgently needed to see her.

Please let it be Nathan. She wanted to avoid Margaret at all costs.

Jessica walked briskly along the harbour to the cafe, following the route that flashed up on the inside of her sunglasses. She'd changed into a pair of white Capri pants and a blue-and-white striped top that helped her blend in with the well-dressed tourists. She also looked suitably "moneyed" if Mr Ingorokva caught sight of her going back on board.

Heart beating rapidly, she entered the cafe. She removed her sunglasses and scanned the dimly lit room, which was lined with large paintings. Most tables were taken; cutlery clattered and the chatter of voices rang out. A waiter brushed past with a large platter of buffalo mozzarella, tomatoes and basil leaves, drizzled with olive oil and sprinkled with pepper. Her stomach growled again. She wanted to grab it off him and wolf down the lot.

Jessica scanned the cafe again; the guests were all ridiculously good-looking. A few people glanced up, but no one tried to catch her eye. She couldn't see

Nathan anywhere – unless he was in disguise. Would he risk showing his face in public when Margaret was in Monaco too?

"Jessica! Over here!"

Her heart sank as she turned around. Margaret sat at a far table, wearing a white sundress. Jessica was used to seeing her in formal trouser suits, but maybe she was trying to look like a tourist. She had a white Liberty scarf knotted at her neck. Some things never changed. Margaret never ditched her scarves, whatever her disguise.

"Are you OK?" Margaret said as she slid into her seat. "You look preoccupied." She pushed a half-eaten plate of salmon pasta to one side and took a sip of sparkling mineral water.

"Hello? Someone tried to kill Kat earlier, or have you forgotten already?" It was poker-face time. She couldn't let Margaret become the least bit suspicious about what she was up to in Monaco.

"There's no need for sarcasm. I'm perfectly aware of what happened – what you *let* happen."

"It wasn't my fault," Jessica retorted. "Or am I supposed to test every piece of food or drink that passes Kat's mouth?"

Margaret stared at her, drumming her pink lacquered fingernails on the table. Was she suspicious? Jessica met her gaze. She had to keep her nerve. Margaret couldn't possibly know anything.

"Stop playing games with me. What was so urgent that you had to drag me away from my dinner? Did you find anything useful back at the hotel?"

Margaret stroked her silk scarf. "It was sulphuric acid, as you suspected, but impossible to trace. It could have been bought at any hardware store in Europe. Background checks on hotel employees have drawn a blank too."

"So whoever did it must be part of Mr Ingorokva's entourage. Have you rechecked the bodyguards and vetted the new tutor, Darya?"

"Of course. I'll let you know if I discover anything, but I'm not hopeful," Margaret said, dismissively. "As I said in my email, we've done a thorough sweep already, and although his employees aren't exactly ones we'd choose for MI6, there's nothing in their backgrounds to suggest they'd be behind the attempted hit."

So Margaret knew that Mr Ingorokva surrounded

himself with the dodgiest people possible.

"We're pursuing a few leads, but in the meantime your brief has changed slightly," Margaret said, taking another sip of water.

"What do you mean? Don't you want me to keep an eye on Kat any more?"

"Oh, yes – now more than ever after what happened today – but I also need you to watch Mr Ingorokva."

Jessica sat back in her chair. Had she heard right? This was remarkably similar to Nathan's instructions. What was Margaret's game?

"Why?" she said evenly. "What's Mr Ingorokva done to annoy you?"

"I don't think he's being completely upfront. It's possible he's engaged in activity that could be detrimental to everyone involved. By which I mean MI6."

Could Margaret be any more vague? "You mean the business deal he's conducting this week? Are you going to tell me what that's all about, or is it still 'need to know'?"

Margaret smiled tightly. "Mr Ingorokva's a slippery

character. I suspect he may be reneging on his deal with MI6. We can't let that happen. The ballot rigging must be stopped. We need to know what he's planning."

Jessica bit her lip. "What am I supposed to do exactly?"

"Report back to me if you hear him discussing any business dealings involving Georgia. You're also ideally placed to have a snoop around his office or other restricted areas."

Jessica flinched slightly, remembering Kat's tour.

"Have you been inside any of those areas already?" Margaret pressed.

Jessica shook her head. "Kat pointed out an area below deck that was restricted access, but there's no way I can get inside. I don't have any gadgets that could bypass the security, remember?"

Drumming her fingers on the table, she stared pointedly at Margaret.

"We all regret the cutbacks at MI6. But you're a very resourceful young lady. I'm sure you'll think of something – for your father's sake."

Jessica held her gaze. Margaret's threats meant nothing now that Nathan had ensured her father's hospital bills would be paid. She could walk away right now if she wanted to, but she didn't. She had to get Margaret.

"Are we done?" Jessica said, scraping her chair as she stood up. "I should get back before I'm missed."

"Of course."

Jessica skirted past her. The meeting hadn't been a total walk in the park, but she'd survived.

"One more thing," Margaret called after her. "Has your father been to visit Nathan lately?"

Jessica stopped. She hadn't escaped that easily.

"No." She turned around. "The hospital told us to stay away; that Nathan is brain-dead and will never recover."

"I received the same message," Margaret said, with a tiny shrug. "It's a little strange. It's not normal hospital policy to keep out family and friends. I double-checked the other day and the lady I spoke to had never heard of Nathan Hall. That's very odd, don't you think?"

Nathan claimed that all hospital staff had been briefed to say exactly the same thing if anyone inquired: no visitors, no comment. Had an agency nurse been omitted from the list of employees MI6 had drawn up?

Jessica stared back coolly. "Maybe she was a new shift worker and didn't know all the patients. A doctor told my dad he'd contact him when visiting hours could be resumed."

"Well do let me know too." Margaret lined up her knife and fork, without looking up. "As I'm sure you realize, I have a very keen interest in Nathan's recovery."

Jessica walked out, face aflame. Had Margaret guessed that Nathan was out of his coma? Both their lives would be in danger if she knew he was in Monaco. They were loose ends she wouldn't hesitate to finish off.

CHAPTER
TEN

Jessica set her alarm for three a.m., which she decided was the best time to explore the yacht without bumping into any patrolling bodyguards. A new, even bigger team had already been employed by Mr Ingorokva, so she needed to be careful.

She dressed in a dark sweater and jeans, and put on her MI6 diamond earrings, watch, necklace and bracelet. There was no way she was going anywhere tonight without her full bling armoury; a would-be killer was loose on the yacht, and she needed to be well equipped at all times. She tossed a few more gadgets into her rucksack, then slipped out of her cabin. She took out the nearby security camera with a spritz of her MI6 hairspray. Within seconds, foam had solidified on the camera lens. It would melt within a couple of hours, leaving no trace it had ever been there. She crept quietly along the corridor, taking out two more cameras.

The restricted area seemed like the best place to start. What did Mr Ingorokva keep down there – apart from his mini submarine and anti-aircraft missile system? She needed to find out, but she'd be reporting the answer back to Nathan, not Margaret.

Jessica paused. Soft footsteps sounded in the corridor ahead. She flung herself against the wall, hardly daring to breathe as a figure, dressed all in black, appeared, ponytail swinging.

Kat!

What was she up to? The trousers, long-sleeved T-shirt and rucksack certainly weren't her usual nightclub gear. Nor was the Halloween zombie mask. Jessica waited a few seconds and then followed. Kat moved quickly in trainers, keeping close to the corridor walls, and stopped as she spotted a camera. Pulling out an aerosol can from her rucksack, she sprinted to the camera and zapped it.

So Kat had come equipped too!

Jessica followed her along the corridor, looking up at the camera as she passed. It was frozen; Kat must have known it could sense heat. Yacht security would never find out – this spray would be melted by morning too. As well as the aerosol, Kat had worn a disguise to dodge the facial-recognition software. She certainly had a few tricks up her sleeve to avoid her bodyguards.

She was up on deck within minutes, with Jessica trailing behind. Tossing the mask in her rucksack, Kat ran down the gangplank without activating a single alarm. This had to be a well-practised route; she'd known how to beat all the cameras. Where was she going? She'd never get admitted to a club or casino dressed like that.

Jessica was about to run after her when another figure appeared. She slammed against the wall and waited a few seconds before peering out again. Darya scurried down the gangplank after her charge. Talk about taking your job seriously. Kat would be in hot water if Darya reported back on tonight's nocturnal activities to Mr Ingorokva.

Jessica followed the two figures from a safe distance. Kat headed into town without a backwards glance. She knew exactly where she was going and didn't hesitate as she navigated the backstreets. She moved fast for someone who said she hated working out. Darya was agile too.

Kat veered on to a deserted one-way street, with her tutor ten metres behind. Jessica turned the corner as Kat leant against a lamp post to catch her breath. Suddenly, she spun around. Jessica threw herself into a shop doorway but Darya wasn't quick enough.

Kat screamed abuse in Russian.

She'd obviously spotted Darya, but had she seen Jessica too? She counted to thirty and peeped out. Darya stood with her back to her, staring down the street, but Kat was long gone.

Jessica traipsed around for the next hour or so, hoping to catch a glimpse of Kat, but only encountered drunks, staggering around after being thrown out of clubs and casinos. Darya had obviously given up too, as she didn't run into her again either.

Heading back to the yacht, she decided she would confront Kat about her secretive little jaunt. She couldn't take risks like that when someone on board was looking for an opportunity to kill her. Jessica kept to the shadows and had almost made it to the door to the lower deck when there was a tiny creak behind her. Before she had time to turn around, she'd crashed to her knees, her head throbbing. She tried to stand up, but her legs didn't work. Something dark and sticky ran down her face. She touched it and stared at her fingers. Was it blood? What had happened?

"Tie her up," a woman commanded.

Jessica tried to speak, but everything slowed down; her tongue was tied in knots and her eyelids were unbelievably heavy. She had to sleep. If it weren't for the loud buzzing in her ears, she could curl up right now and blank everything out. The deck lurched and there was a loud crack as she fell face down. She didn't feel anything. Her face was totally numb, but she registered that her cheek was pressed against the deck, blood pooling by her mouth.

Someone was manhandling her, tying her hands and feet tightly together with tape. Blood filled her mouth. She coughed it out.

"What now?" a man said.

His voice sounded distant as if he were talking at the end of a very long tunnel.

"Throw her overboard."

"That's not what I'm being paid to do. She could help us find it. We can make her talk."

"Are you the boss or am I?" the woman snarled. "Throw the Cole brat overboard before she fights back."

Jessica tried to lift her head. How did the woman know her name? Her voice sounded vaguely familiar.

"She's not going anywhere. You're not my boss, remember? I don't take orders from you." His voice was muffled by something. A scarf, maybe?

There was a rustling noise. "I won't hesitate to pull the trigger unless you do exactly as I say. The brat has to die."

"No! Help me!" Jessica screamed but the words came out as barely a whisper.

Hands heaved her up and she was thrown over someone's shoulder. She tried to focus, but the buzzing noise in her ears grew louder and louder. The pain in her head was unbearable. Her hands dangled down the man's back. He was wearing jeans and white trainers.

She saw another pair of legs close by, clad in dark trousers and black court shoes.

"You won't cheat death this time," the woman whispered in her ear. "I'll be sure to send a sympathy card to your father and Mattie."

Jessica's blood ran cold. She recognized the voice through the fog in her head.

"Allegra," she breathed. "Allegra Knight."

It was the madwoman who'd wanted to seriously injure teenagers with her doctored face cream, and had tried to kill her and her dad in Paris.

"Goodbye. We won't meet again."

"You don't have to do this," Jessica mumbled. "I won't tell anyone you're here. I promise."

Allegra chuckled. "Where's the fun in that? You won't dodge death again. Your nine lives are up."

"I'm telling you this is a mistake," the man said. "These aren't our orders. Let me give her some truth serum and interrogate her. She'll give up what she knows."

"No!"

Hands roughly grabbed Jessica and yanked her off the man's shoulder. As she tipped headfirst over the railings, she caught a glimpse of a woman staring back at her from the depths, her strawberry-blonde hair splayed out, Medusa-like. Was that her mum?

The cold water sliced into her body, shocking her senses back to life. Her eyes flew open as she sank. It wasn't her mum's face staring at her from the water; it was her own reflection. Blood swirled in front of her face, blinding her. She panicked and swallowed water. She tried to move her arms and legs, but they were tightly pinned together. Kicking feebly, she managed to slow her descent, but her legs weren't strong enough to get her back to the surface. She was going to drown. She could hold her breath for another minute and that would be it.

She couldn't struggle any more; her lungs were crushed. As she sank, something hard knocked against her face and her eyes flew open. The necklace! Nathan said if she bit into it, she'd get seven minutes worth of oxygen. It was enough to get her to the surface.

Jessica opened her mouth, swallowing more water as she attempted to reach the pendant. She caught it between her teeth on the second attempt and bit down hard. There was a hissing sensation as water was expelled through the side of her mouth. She could breathe! The pain in her lungs melted away. If she continued to breathe through her mouth instead of her nose, she'd make it.

Now she had to get out of her binds. She was still sinking. If she didn't do something pronto she'd die anyway, as she couldn't swim to the surface while tied up. She swivelled around and kicked her legs through her hands, bringing her arms out in front of her body. Spitting out the pendant, she bit into the fob on the side of her Rolex.

Once activated, she caught the silver object between her teeth again and sucked in more oxygen. She tucked her legs up beneath her and directed the watch at the tape. The laser sliced through the plastic, releasing her feet. She kicked, but was feeling much weaker. She looked up. The surface was clouded with blood. She had to get there before she passed out.

As she kicked, she blasted the tape around her hands. Pain seared through her wrist as she accidentally hit her skin. Her hands finally broke apart and she clawed her way upwards. The light from the yacht shimmered enticingly. It was so close, but exhaustion gripped her again.

She gave one last desperate kick and broke through the water, taking in a huge breath. She floated helplessly on her back. She couldn't feel her arms or legs. Oh God. She'd made it to the surface but was still going to drown. She had no idea if Allegra was still on board the yacht, but she had to take the risk and try to raise the alarm.

"Help!" Jessica cried. "Someone, help!"

Water filled her eyes and mouth as she sank. She spluttered up again. She looked up at the stars, which seemed so close that she reached out to touch them. Was her mum staring down at her right now? Jessica closed her eyes as water splashed into her nostrils. She could see her mum's face again. She smiled at her.

"Jessica!" a voice shouted. "She's in the water. Someone help her!"

A flash of light blinded her. There was a loud splash and a few seconds later someone tugged roughly at her arm and forced an inflatable over her shoulders. She was dragged through the water towards the yacht and winched upwards on to something hard. Loud voices pierced her eardrums.

"Mum?" Jessica whispered. "Is that you?"

She lay on her back, transfixed by the stars. They followed her wherever she stared.

"No, it's Kat," a voice said close to her ear. "Stay with me, Jessica. You're safe now. I found you."

CHAPTER
ELEVEN

Jessica was back on the deck again, lying face down in a pool of blood. This time she could swivel around and see her attackers.

"Throw her overboard! Kill her now!" Becky stepped forward, her face distorted with hatred.

"Stop, Becky! We're friends, remember?"

"Do as I say," Becky said.

Her accomplice tossed Jessica over his shoulder.

"Sorry it didn't work out between us," Jamie said, laughing. "But I've moved on. Consider this closure."

He tipped her over the yacht's railings.

"AAAAGH!"

*

Jessica's eyes flew open as she shot up in bed. Bright lights flashed, making her head explode with pain. She sank back into the pillow in a daze.

"Easy does it," a male voice said. "Try not to make any sudden movements or you'll pass out again."

She blinked and tried to focus. A blurry figure stood by the bed. And another. And another. It was hard to tell how many people were in front of her. They jumped about all over the place. Why were they doing that?

"Go away! Don't hurt me!" Her head felt like it could split in two.

"You're safe. I'm Dr Fedorovna; you're in the medical centre on board Mr Ingorokva's yacht. What happened to you?"

"Was attacked..." Jessica mumbled. "Thrown overboard..."

She eased herself up on to the pillow. She could focus on the doctor now. Another figure appeared and leaned threateningly over her. The room started to swim again.

"Who did this to you?" a voice growled. "Tell me!"

Jessica closed her eyes, feeling nauseous. "A man and woman."

"Please step back. I don't think Jessica's up to answering questions right now."

"She has to," Mr Ingorokva insisted. "What language did they speak? Russian? English?"

Jessica bit her lip. She might throw up at any minute.

"Both English," she whispered.

"Did they say anything that could identify them? Anything at all?"

She couldn't tell Mr Ingorokva the truth. One of her attackers was definitely Allegra Knight who'd tried to kill her before. What was she doing here in Monaco? The man had said he didn't take orders from Allegra. But if not her, who? It sounded like someone else was involved. Had Allegra joined forces with Margaret again?

"That's enough questions for now, sir," Dr Fedorovna said firmly. "Jessica needs to rest."

"Do I have to remind you that I'm your employer?" Mr Ingorokva hit back.

"And I'm Jessica's doctor. Her care has to be my first priority. She's been through a terrible trauma. She could have been killed tonight."

"I need to know. I don't have time to waste."

Jessica winced as the men argued loudly.

"Please come back later," Dr Fedorovna said. "She can answer your questions when she's better."

Jessica opened her eyes to see Mr Ingorokva being led out, still protesting. Kat gave her a small smile as she passed her handbag. "Your mobile's inside. I thought you might want to call someone."

"Thank you," Jessica said, holding it tightly. "You saved my life. You came back."

Kat reddened and slipped out after her dad without another word.

"I'm sorry about that," Dr Fedorovna said, striding back. "I couldn't keep them out any longer. I administered a local anaesthetic to stitch your head wound, but these pills should help with the pain and make you sleep. You're lucky there's no concussion."

He handed her a small plastic cup containing four tablets. She put them in her mouth but kept them under her tongue as she took a gulp of water.

"I'll check on you every couple of hours. Is there anyone you want me to ring?"

Jessica shook her head. "I can do it, thanks."

She waited until he'd left the room before searching her handbag. She'd left her iPad in the cabin and didn't want to risk using her mobile, which Margaret could have tapped. Unzipping her make-up bag, she took out the eyeshadow palette, which masked a mini-computer.

Allegra Knight's in Monaco, she typed to Nathan. *Tried to kill me with male accomplice. Find her.* She swallowed the pills and sank back into her pillow.

Nathan had to act quickly. Once Allegra realized Jessica had survived, she'd come back to finish the job.

CHAPTER
TWELVE

"You've been out, like, *forever*," a voice said accusingly. "I've had to sunbathe alone all day. It's been a total drag."

Jessica's eyes flew open. She looked about the white room. Kat sat next to her, flicking through *Teen Vogue*. She stood up and dumped a large pile of magazines on the bed, fanning through them. Jessica caught sight of *Hello!* and *National Geographic*.

"I didn't know which magazines you liked best, so Papa bought them all," Kat said, with a shrug. "I've got some more of your things too." She pointed to a vanity case in the corner. "I found these sunglasses in your cabin."

What on earth had got into Kat? Had she been

abducted by aliens and replaced by her nice identical twin? She'd saved her life and was now trying to make her as comfortable as possible. Jessica examined the MI6 glasses.

"Thank you, again. For saving me."

As she eased herself up the bed, Kat sprang forward to adjust the pillows.

"There. That's better, isn't it?"

"What is it, Kat?" Jessica said, rubbing her forehead. "You're being way too nice to me. What do you want?" She noticed that Dr Fedorovna had left more painkillers on her bedside table. She knocked back a couple with a glass of water.

"Nothing," she replied innocently. "I just wanted to make sure you're OK."

"It's kind of you to be so concerned, and I'm grateful for everything you've done, but Dr Fedorovna said I needed to rest. So if you don't mind." Jessica glanced pointedly at the door.

Resting was the last thing on her mind; she desperately wanted to check in with Nathan to see if he'd made any progress in tracking down Allegra and her accomplice.

"Oh, don't worry about Andrei," Kat said breezily. "He's gone for a cigarette, so we've got time before he comes back. I thought we could talk." She picked up Jessica's sunglasses again from the bed and examined them closely. "Cool glasses by the way. They're different to the ones you had on the plane."

"That pair hasn't turned up yet."

"I expect a cleaner stole them. You know what some of them are like."

Jessica didn't have the energy to challenge her. She watched as Kat tried on the glasses and admired herself in the mirror.

"I love your watch too." She held the Rolex up to the light. "I thought it was a fake the first time I saw it, but it's not, is it? It's the real thing." She fastened it on her wrist. "How did you manage to afford something so expensive?"

"Birthday present," Jessica said bluntly. "What did you want to talk about?"

"Oh." Kat removed the watch and sunglasses and put them back on the table. "Why, about what happened last night, of course. Do you think whoever attacked you could have sent death threats to me?"

"Er, what death threats?" She couldn't let on she knew all about the letters. Kat would immediately want to know who'd told her.

Kat shuddered. "I found some notes in Papa's office a while ago. He must have received more because he's ramped up my security. He thinks he can protect me but he can't, and whoever's doing this is getting closer. They put sulphuric acid in my drink at the hotel and must have attacked you by mistake last night."

"They didn't think it was you. They were definitely after me."

Jessica remembered Allegra's words: "throw the Cole brat overboard".

Kat looked a little disappointed. "Why would someone want to kill you? It's not like you're worth anything."

Jessica raised an eyebrow. "Cheers."

"Well, you know what I mean," she said hastily. "Money-wise. It seems strange that someone would attack you when you're only a model and don't have any connection to my family. I mean, you're not living some kind of double life that I don't know about, are you?"

Kat scrutinized her face.

"Of course not," Jessica said, without blinking.

"It's just that. . ." Her voice trailed off. She stared at the sunglasses again.

"What?"

"Why were you following me around Monaco last night?"

So Kat *had* spotted her. That was what she was fretting about; whether she was going to snitch to her dad.

"I heard a noise outside my cabin and went to investigate. I saw you leaving the yacht and thought you were probably heading somewhere cool, like a club. I wanted to tag along."

Kat's eyes narrowed. "Didn't you wonder why I was dressed like that?"

"It did cross my mind." Kat was definitely a lot sharper than anyone, including her dad, gave her credit for.

"I can move faster in trainers, but my dress and strappy shoes were in my rucksack. Papa can't find out though. He'd kill me if he knew I went ashore at night."

"It's risky. What if you'd bumped into whoever you say is threatening you?"

"I'm not afraid." Kat's voice faltered a little.

Behind the bravado, Jessica knew Kat was scared. She should be. But there was no point pushing it; she'd never admit to being frightened.

"You lost me pretty quickly. How did you manage that?"

Kat laughed. "Practice, of course. I'm used to dodging my bodyguards."

Hhhm. Jessica eyed her suspiciously. Kat was lying about something, she was sure. "So how was it?"

"How was what?"

"The club, of course, or wherever you went."

"It was a casino actually, and it was a bit of a drag so I came back early. That's when I saw you in the water and raised the alarm – one of the crew saved you, and he promised not to tell Papa I was there. As far as he knows, I heard a commotion in the corridor and came up on deck to see what was happening. That's when I found Dr Fedorovna doing CPR on you."

Jessica closed her eyes and was immediately back in

the freezing water, fighting to get out. Panic rose in her throat, choking her.

"Jessica?"

She opened her eyes and exhaled. She hadn't realized she was holding her breath.

"If it hadn't been for you, I'd have drowned."

"So I guess you owe me," Kat said brightly. "That means you have to promise not to breathe a word about last night to Papa."

"Sure thing." She'd much prefer not having to broach Kat's secretive little jaunt to Mr Ingorokva. She hadn't forgotten the gun in his office drawer.

"Excellent!" Kat beamed. "Let's not discuss it again. I've got some exciting news to fill you in on: my hand's miles better, I've got a new shoot lined up in Tokyo next week, and I'm down to the last three for a new mascara campaign. The casting's in London. Oh, and by the way, Papa had to let Darya go."

Jessica rolled her eyes. This had to be Kat's preventive strike before Darya could spill the beans about what she'd seen. As a new, senior employee, she'd be obliged to report Kat's night-time trip to Mr

Ingorokva. Kat would have had far more trouble trying to persuade *her* to keep quiet.

"Wow. That's convenient. And quick. How did you manage it?"

Kat blushed a deep crimson. "I had nothing to do with it. While I was out last night Darya broke into my cabin and stole my Fabergé egg."

"No way!"

"It's true. She must have taken it while I was ashore. When I got back it was gone. Papa imposed a lockdown and searched the yacht from top to bottom. It was found hidden in a bag in Darya's wardrobe."

"That doesn't make any sense. We both know she followed you off the yacht."

Kat sniffed. "Well, she did it when she got back to spite me."

"Why would she risk doing something as stupid as that? She must have known she'd get caught. If she'd taken something so valuable, she'd have got it off the yacht as soon as possible and vanished."

Kat glared at her. "How should I know what was going on in that idiot's head? She wasn't the brightest tool in the box. The egg's worth millions. Maybe

Darya was tempted. She heard us talking about the egg at breakfast and how it'd be in my room for one night before being locked in Papa's safe. She must have realized she only had one chance to steal it."

"I thought you said she couldn't speak English?" Jessica pointed out. "She couldn't have understood what was being said at breakfast."

"Enough!" Kat shouted.

Jessica winced, the noise slicing through her head.

Kat's lips curled into an ugly scowl. She sounded exactly like her dad when she was angry. "I'm telling you what happened, so accept it and don't start making waves by telling Papa anything different."

Jessica glared back. "You could have found another excuse to get rid of Darya. You didn't have to falsely accuse her of theft. She could struggle to find work after this."

Kat's nostrils flared. "I have no idea what you're talking about."

"I think you do," she countered. "It's low to get someone fired to cover your own back."

Kat glowered at her. "Maybe you should watch *your* back. I can get rid of you just as easily."

"I never doubted it. Not for a minute."

Kat swept the magazines off the bed and slammed the door behind her. Jessica stared after her. Kat was as ruthless as her dad; an Ingorokva through and through.

CHAPTER
THIRTEEN

Sunlight streamed into the cabin, warming Jessica's cheeks. She peeled her eyes open and glanced at the clock. It was eight a.m. She'd slept most of yesterday after Kat's fiery visit. She'd given Mr Ingorokva a basic account of being hit over the head and thrown overboard, and his security team was investigating. Nathan had advised her by email to keep it simple and not to mention Allegra Knight's involvement. She hadn't filled Margaret in on the whole story either. What was the point? She probably already knew Allegra was in Monaco – she might even have masterminded the attack – and she certainly didn't sound too worried when she emailed back. She was more interested in hearing if she'd found out anything useful about Mr Ingorokva's business dealings.

Jessica looked up as the door swung open. Dr Fedorovna walked in, holding a newspaper. He smiled broadly at her. "How are you feeling?"

"Much better, thanks. My head doesn't feel as if it's going to fall off my body any more."

"Good. You have half a dozen stitches in your head which should dissolve within a couple of days. They shouldn't scar. I'd recommend you take it easy and rest if you still want to take part in the fashion show tomorrow. I've got more painkillers if you need them."

"It feels OK at the moment, but I am hungry."

"I'll get some breakfast brought to you straight away," he said, passing her the newspaper. "Any preferences?"

"Scrambled egg on toast would be great."

Dr Fedorovna rang the kitchen while she scanned the local paper.

HAS THE CAT BURGLAR STRUCK AGAIN?

A thief has escaped with diamond jewellery worth over five million euros following a daring heist at a top Monaco hotel last night.

167

The burglar struck as shipping heiress Isabelle St Valerie slept in her suite at the Hotel Hermitage.

The intruder gained access to her locked room and made away with a stash including a pair of antique diamond earrings, a sapphire bracelet and an emerald necklace.

The raid bears striking similarities to a burglary in Monaco three months ago when jewellery was snatched from the dressing table of a wealthy American widow as she slept. Again, the door to her suite was locked.

Police said they are keeping an open mind about whether the two thefts are connected. Both women had been pictured wearing their jewels in newspaper diary columns in Monaco, prior to the raids.

A source close to the inquiry said: "It would appear that the cat burglar has struck again. We believe they knew exactly who to target."

"The famous cat burglar," Dr Fedorovna said, strolling over. "He never leaves a trace, wherever he goes."

"I guess Monaco attracts crooks as well as the filthy rich," Jessica said.

"Sometimes they're one and the same." Dr Fedorovna felt her pulse and checked her blood pressure. "Not everyone in Monaco is what they seem."

"I guess." Jessica glanced back at the paper. Did the theft have anything to do with Allegra? Maybe her male accomplice was the culprit. They were certainly looking for something on board *Lilya*. Could they have been after Kat's Fabergé egg or her jewellery? She didn't believe Kat's story that Darya was a thief.

"I'll take a look at your hand before I leave you in peace." Dr Fedorovna unpeeled the bandage. "Do you have any idea how you did this?"

Jessica shuddered at the sight of scorched flesh. "I don't remember much."

The pain from the laser had been agonizing, but she'd been able to use her hand to get to the surface. Thank God Allegra hadn't been waiting for her on deck. Where was she now? Could she be hiding on the yacht somewhere? She shouldn't rule out that possibility; Allegra had managed to slip on board relatively easily.

"I'm sorry. Did I hurt you?"

"No. It's OK." Jessica bit her lip as Dr Fedorovna examined the red marks around her wrists.

"I have to admit, I'm curious," he said. "How did you get out of your constraints underwater?"

"What?"

"Your arms and legs were tied."

Jessica tried not to flinch. She hadn't mentioned the constraints to anyone apart from Nathan. How did Dr Fedorovna know? Could he tell from the faint red marks on her skin? She glanced down at his feet and froze. He was wearing white trainers. Was that a spot of blood by the heel? *Her* blood?

"I was panicking and pulling at the ties around my wrists," she said quickly. "I guess they came loose in the water."

"You were very lucky. I'm sure you realize that."

"I do." Jessica's heart raced. She was too weak to put up much of a fight if he realized she'd identified him. He'd claimed he had access to a truth serum, but what else did he have in the medical centre? Poison?

170

Dr Fedorovna gazed down at her for what felt like an age.

"I have some errands to run in town, but I'll check on you in a bit. You can go up on deck if you feel up to it, but wear these." He passed her sunglasses from the bedside table. "Doctor's orders. It's a hot day. You don't want a headache from the sun on top of everything else, do you?"

Jessica put them on and squeezed out a smile as she slid off the bed. "There. Happy?"

"Very stylish."

She took a sharp breath and whipped the glasses off again.

"Did you stand up too quickly? Do you feel dizzy?" Dr Fedorovna was at her side. "I can stay if you want." He checked her pulse again and frowned.

Could he sense her panic? She had to get rid of him. "No, I'm fine. I feel better now." She smiled brightly. "Go and do what you have to do. I'm good. I'll get dressed and go and find Kat. She's been moaning about sunbathing alone."

The doctor checked his watch. "If you're absolutely sure."

Jessica nodded vigorously.

"Well, I am running a bit late. I'll be back in half an hour."

She waited until the door clicked shut behind him before putting the glasses back on. Either she'd forgotten to turn off the program the last time she'd used them or Kat had accidentally switched it on. The MI6 glasses had automatically carried out a facial recognition check on Dr Fedorovna. Except that wasn't his real name; no one knew what it was as he used at least a dozen aliases. He was a Russian hitman who was wanted by MI6 for the contract killing of three Moscow businessmen in London.

:CHAPTER:
FOURTEEN

Jessica threw her clothes on before the imposter returned. Had Allegra hired him to attack her? She couldn't have thrown Jessica overboard herself; she wasn't strong enough. Allegra needed help and a person on the inside was ideally placed to alert her to Jessica's movements. Maybe he'd seen her up on deck, following Kat, and waited to ambush her when she returned. But who else knew he was here? Margaret said she'd carried out checks on all Mr Ingorokva's employees. Did she know the doctor's real identity? Did Mr Ingorokva? It was unlikely *he'd* deliberately put Kat in the crossfire of a dangerous assassin. This "Fake Fed" could be targeting Kat. He had to be a prime suspect.

Jessica fired up her iPad and placed her sunglasses next to it to find a wireless connection. Nathan had warned her not to trawl through MI6 files unless absolutely necessary, but this had to be worth the risk. Within seconds, she was in and had downloaded Fake Fed's faceprint and files on to her iPad. The doctor had first registered on MI6's radar at the age of twenty-four, when he was working for the KGB under the alias "Boris Andreyki". MI6 believed he'd trained in medicine, possibly graduating from Stalingrad University, and was suspected of carrying out at least four assassinations of "enemies of the state", including journalists and business moguls, while working in his day job as an emergency-room doctor.

MI6 had very little on him from the age of twenty-six onwards, but he'd resurfaced a few years ago under another pseudonym, "Boris Ibramowich", carrying out a hit on three Russian businessmen in London. He was then believed to have gone rogue and become an assassin for hire, with clients including Vectra.

Jessica ran her hands through her hair. It didn't make any sense. If Fake Fed had been hired to kill Kat, what was he waiting for? He must have had lots of opportunities, especially since Kat kept trying to find excuses to be alone with him. Surely it would have been easy to poison her in the medical centre instead of going to the trouble of lacing her drink with sulphuric acid at the hotel? That was a far riskier strategy and much more likely to fail, which it had.

Also, if he'd been with Allegra last night, why was he so reluctant to throw her overboard? Allegra had taken over at the crucial moment. He'd proven himself to be ruthless by the number of people he'd killed, but had he drawn the line at killing a teenage girl, or did his mission on board the yacht not involve murdering Jessica? He'd wanted to pump her for information, but Allegra had forced him to act.

What was he after?

Jessica typed "Dr Andrei Fedorovna", the real Dr Fedorovna, into the database and gasped as an image appeared on the screen. The doctor was in his seventies, with a white beard and glasses. He was also dead – found six months ago with his throat slashed in his apartment in Brazil, where he'd owned a private healthcare company and managed an exclusive plastic surgery clinic. According to the MI6 file, he had connections with drugs cartels, one of which was believed to be behind his murder.

Jessica bit her nail. What if MI6 was wrong, and this imposter had murdered the real Dr Fedorovna so he could assume his identity and carry out the hit on Kat? Mr Ingorokva would have been impressed by the doctor's list of credentials; she could imagine him boasting about how Dr Fedorovna ran his own clinics in South America without checking further.

He had to be warned before the hitman returned. She tapped out a message to Nathan on her eyeshadow palette, grabbed her handbag and ran. She didn't have time to wait for his reply.

Jessica slid to a halt outside Mr Ingorokva's office. The new bodyguards must have been on shift change because no one was guarding the room. That was odd; he usually surrounded himself with security at all times. The door was slightly ajar and a voice boomed out. Jessica peered through the gap; Mr Ingorokva was standing with his back turned, talking loudly in Russian. Jessica rummaged in her handbag, retrieved the iPod nano, and stuck the earphones in.

They buzzed with static so she carefully moved closer, opening the door a fraction of an inch wider. This time his words rang clearly in her ears as the iPod translated him instantaneously.

"This little mishap doesn't alter our plans. MI6 won't get in the way. Margaret Becker knows nothing, and I plan to keep it that way. She's distracted with averting the ballot rigging. We'll go ahead as arranged."

He fell silent, listening to the other person.

"Stop worrying," he barked back. "Of course I still have the weapon. It's well hidden on board. A guest disturbed whoever had been sent to steal it. The question is are you still good for 800 million euros?"

Jessica caught her breath. Allegra and Fake Fed had been looking for a weapon, not the Fabergé egg or jewels. Was this the real reason that Margaret was so interested in arranging protection for Kat? Maybe she'd discovered Mr Ingorokva's dirty little secret and was after the weapon too.

"I'll bring the briefcase tomorrow night as planned," he continued. "Don't be late. Eleven p.m., sharp. Security will be tight at the palace, but I've ensured your name is on the accredited list."

Jessica took a step back. The meet was at the Grimaldi Palace, after the fashion show. Talk about devious. Mr Ingorokva had arranged the spectacle as a front for his arms deal, not to make Kat happy or to keep up Jessica's cover story. It was a high-security venue and guests would have been vetted weeks in advance. It'd be the perfect cover for the exchange with his buyer; he'd be surrounded by security guards. The guests wouldn't realize what was taking place right in front of their noses.

"Is someone there?" Mr Ingorokva paused for a few seconds. "Call me back. I have to go."

Oh, no! Jessica fell back a step, panicking. Running away or hiding wasn't an option. His bodyguards had appeared at the end of the corridor. They clocked her as soon as they turned the corner. When Mr Ingorokva's footsteps reached the door, Jessica's hand was already raised as if she were about to knock. She'd have to blag her way out of this one. The door flung open.

"You!" he thundered. "How long have you been standing there?"

"Er, not long."

"Have you been eavesdropping on me for Margaret? Is that why you're here?" He grabbed her arm roughly and shook it.

"No, of course not. Let go of me." She yanked her arm free. "I realized you were on the phone and thought I'd wait until you finished. I need to speak to you urgently."

Mr Ingorokva glared at her. "Katyenka says you don't speak any Russian. Is that true?"

"Not exactly. Another Russian model taught me a few phrases like 'good morning' and 'my name is Jessica', but that's about it. I'm not exactly fluent."

Mr Ingorokva stared hard. Without warning, he snatched the iPod out of her hand. He tossed it over to one of his bodyguards who examined it carefully.

"Hey! What do you think you're doing? That's mine!"

The guard flicked it on, pumping out Kesha.

"Not that dreadful music again." Mr Ingorokva sighed. "Don't teenagers listen to anything else these days?"

Jessica ignored his question. "Can I have it back, please?"

Mr Ingorokva nodded at the guard, who threw it over with a smirk.

"You must understand that I have to be careful. You'd be surprised by the lengths my enemies will go to discover my business. These sorts of things can be planted with bugs, you know." He gestured to the iPod.

Jessica slipped it back in her bag. "It's news to me. Margaret said MI6 couldn't afford to give me any gadgets."

He studied her face for what felt like an age. "What did you want to see me about?"

She took a deep breath. "I think Dr Fedorovna may be behind the threats on Kat's life. How carefully did you vet him?"

"What?" Mr Ingorokva stroked his moustache. "My head of security checked out his credentials. He's a fully qualified doctor from South America. He runs his own company."

"Yes, the real Dr Fedorovna is fully qualified, but he was murdered in Brazil six months ago."

His face whitened. "How do you know?"

"I found a newspaper report about the real Dr

Fedorovna online. I don't know who your doctor is," Jessica lied. "But it's not Dr Andrei Fedorovna."

Jessica could tell by the look on his face that he had no idea the doctor was an imposter. She couldn't reveal he was a hitman in case Mr Ingorokva spoke to Margaret. She'd wonder how Jessica had managed to find out classified information about him.

"Did he have access to your jet in New York?" Jessica asked.

"The pilot needed medication and the doctor administered it on board. Then he flew to Monaco with our staff on another plane."

"So he would have had time to plant the death threat against Kat in your private quarters?"

Mr Ingorokva paused. "He wasn't accompanied by a guard. He could have gone anywhere on my jet."

"He had the perfect opportunity to strike," Jessica said. "He's ashore at the moment, but you can't risk him being near Kat again. You need to call the police straight away."

"No!"

"But I think—"

"Leave now!" Mr Ingorokva thundered. "I will deal with him myself."

Jessica shivered. He hadn't wanted to involve the police after her attack. She remembered the gun in his drawer. How could she have been so stupid? She should have waited for Nathan's orders before telling him. If he killed Fake Fed in a fit of rage, they'd never find out who'd hired him or what he and Allegra were planning to do with the weapon.

"Come in!" he shouted.

Two bodyguards pushed past, throwing her off balance.

Mr Ingorokva barked an order in Russian. One of the men grabbed Jessica's arm and marched her to the door.

"Hey!" she cried. "Let go!"

The guard shoved her backwards and slammed the door. The message was clear: they were going to deal with the doctor their way. Why hadn't she waited? Nathan would be furious with her. He could have had Fake Fed arrested and interrogated.

Uh-oh. Kat. Someone had to break the news about her beloved doctor; she wouldn't take it well. No doubt she was sunning herself up on deck. Jessica ran along the corridor. Her phone buzzed with a text message as she climbed the stairs. Hopefully it was Nathan telling her he'd intercepted Fake Fed dockside, averting a total bloodbath on board.

She checked her phone and didn't recognize the mobile number. There was an attachment but no message. She clicked it open. *What?* She stared numbly at the photo.

Becky and Jamie were kissing.

She shook her head as she slumped to her knees. It was impossible. Becky wouldn't do this to her. Neither would Jamie. Or would they? Was this the real reason they weren't returning her calls or texts? Were they too ashamed to speak to her after stabbing her in the back? She couldn't think straight. She hit "BFF".

Becky picked up after a few rings. She sounded like she was on the Underground again.

"Hello?"

"How could you?" she demanded.

"Er, what? Is that you, Jessica?"

"Of course it's me. I can't believe you'd do that."

"What *are* you talking about?"

"Don't deny it. I saw the photo of you and Jamie kissing."

"Calm down." Becky shouted over a train announcement in the background. "It's not what you think. I can explain."

"Don't bother," Jessica said, her hand trembling. "Photos don't lie."

"You're wrong. Let me—"

"No! Leave me alone."

She hung up and staggered to her feet. She couldn't deal with this right now. Allegra was somewhere in Monaco, intent on murdering her, and a hitman was returning to the yacht any minute. She had to find Kat.

CHAPTER
FIFTEEN

Jessica froze as she reached the top deck; She saw Kat sunbathing in a black bikini on a recliner. Fake Fed was perched on the edge of another sunlounger, unwinding the bandage from her hand. Kat repositioned herself, playing with a tendril of hair and attempting to make eye contact, but the imposter concentrated on examining her acid wound.

"Kat!" Jessica called over. "Can you come here, please?"

She stared over the top of her sunglasses. "No! Can't you see I'm busy? Andrei's checking my hand."

The fake doctor jumped to his feet. "Is everything all right? I was about to come and see you when Kat said her wound needed urgent attention."

Out the corner of her eye, Jessica noticed Mr Ingorokva's bodyguards edging closer.

"You need to come below deck, Kat," she said urgently. "Right now!"

"Why? What's wrong?" She took off her sunglasses and sat up, squinting at Jessica.

"Do it, Kat."

Fake Fed stared at Jessica and then at the approaching bodyguards. He took a step backwards as Mr Ingorokva appeared, grim-faced. The doctor's hand reached into his jacket.

"No!" Jessica charged at him. She roundhouse kicked his arm as he pulled out a gun and aimed at Mr Ingorokva. His hand jerked back as her shin bone cracked against his wrist. She spun round and grabbed him by the shoulders, aiming her knee at his stomach. The gun slipped from his grasp and the bodyguards jumped on him, pounding him to the deck.

"Stop it! Stop!" Kat screamed. She pummelled a bodyguard with her fists.

Mr Ingorokva swung around in a fury. His eyes met Jessica's. "Take Kat below deck," he yelled. "Now!"

Jessica grabbed Kat and shoved her towards the

door as the bodyguards hauled the hitman to his feet. He shouted abuse in Russian at Mr Ingorokva, eyes bulging with fury and spit bubbling at the side of his mouth.

Jessica watched as they bundled him down the gangplank towards a waiting black Merc. Mr Ingorokva opened the passenger door and pushed Fake Fed inside, sending him sprawling, then jumped in and pulled the door shut. The Merc sped away, tyres squealing.

"What's going on?" Kat wailed. "Why did Andrei pull a gun on Papa?"

"I overheard your dad speaking to the bodyguards below deck. He said the real Dr Fedorovna's dead and that man's an imposter. Your dad thinks he's behind the death threats."

"No!" Kat cried. "That's impossible. It's not him."

"You saw him point a gun at your dad. He was prepared to pull the trigger. He could have taken you out next."

"He'd never do that!" Kat whipped out her mobile and dialled a number. "I'm going to ring Papa right now and tell him there's been a big mistake. Andrei was defending himself from Papa's bodyguards. Everyone knows they're thugs."

"I know you fancy him," Jessica said, "but you have to face facts. Think about it, Kat. Why would a doctor carry a gun? It doesn't make any sense."

"Working for Papa is a dangerous job. Someone could try and kill him."

"Or maybe your dad's right and *he's* the dangerous one. He could have paid someone in the hotel to slip sulphuric acid into your drink. He has access to your dad and could plant death threats quite easily."

Kat shook her head violently. "You're wrong. Whatever bad blood there is between him and Papa, he didn't have anything to do with the threats against me."

"How can you be so sure?"

"Because he's kind, sweet and caring."

"I know it's hard to hear, but it looks like it's been an act to get close to you," Jessica said gently. "So he could hurt you."

"He'd never hurt me," Kat said, sobbing. "You don't know him the way I do. I love him."

"You're fourteen."

"So what? Juliet was almost fourteen when she fell in love with Romeo."

"Yes, but—" Jessica stopped herself. Fake Fed was *so* not Romeo in this scenario, but there was no getting through to Kat. "Have you actually told him that you love him?"

"Of course not. Do you think I'm crazy?"

"Yes, pretty much."

Kat glared at her. "It's not what you think. Nothing ever happened between us, but one day when I'm grown up and he's..." Her voice trailed off as she dialled her dad. "Dammit. Papa's phone is switched off. What do you think he's going to do with him?"

"I have no idea, but it doesn't involve the police. That's not your dad's way."

"I have to stop this," Kat said, rubbing her forehead. "I have to find out where they're taking him. I know I can make this right. Papa will listen to me if he'll only pick up."

"I understand that you're upset but you need to stay out of this – for your own safety." Jessica touched her shoulder. "It's too dangerous."

"Get your hands off me," she hissed. "This is your

189

fault. You've been whispering lies in Papa's ear to punish me for getting Darya sacked."

"No, I haven't! It's not like that!"

"What is it like, then? Are you jealous of my relationship with Andrei? Do you want him for yourself? I'll get you for this. I hate you!"

Kat stormed away, knocking into a man carrying a tray of iced drinks.

"Watch where you're going, you klutz!" she shrieked, as the glasses smashed on to the deck.

She stormed through the door to lower deck, slamming it behind her. Jessica caught the man's arm as the liquid pooled on the decking. Could this be another assassination attempt by Fake Fed? The wood darkened but didn't start to disintegrate; it wasn't sulphuric acid. She crouched down to help pick up the shards of glass.

She'd unmasked the culprit – almost getting killed in the process – which meant Mr Ingorokva would send her home soon, possibly as early as tomorrow. But she'd have to find a way to stall; she wasn't ready to leave Monaco yet. There had to be a way to nail Margaret.

CHAPTER
SIXTEEN

Jessica swung from the yacht's railings, stretching her arm over the water. Her diamonds glittered in the sunlight as she worked angle after angle, trying her hardest to make it up to Lucas, the photographer, after forgetting about his pre-ball shoot. She'd been busy filing a detailed report to Nathan about the conversation she'd overheard outside Mr Ingorokva's office, the weapon deal at the ball and the unmasking of Fake Fed.

Jessica had arrived forty-five minutes late, sweating from running in the heat and sporting bruises and cuts. It wasn't a good look. The make-up artist had almost had a heart attack, and spent a good fifteen minutes discussing with the stylist how best to conceal her injuries, which delayed the shoot even more. At least she'd turned up. Kat had refused point-blank to come along and was sulking in her cabin.

The stylist had finally settled on a white Gucci swimsuit, with a long white Missoni kaftan on top, which helpfully covered the red marks on her arms and legs, together with heavy make-up. The hairstylist managed to hide the stitches in her head with a hairpiece and diamond clip.

"That's beautiful!" Lucas shouted. "Now lean back a little more . . . a little more."

Tipping backwards off the *Meridian*, Jessica had a flashback to being thrown off Mr Ingorokva's yacht.

"Relax your mouth – it's tensing up," the photographer ordered.

Jessica pushed the thoughts from her head and went back into "work mode", making sure the sunlight hit her face at exactly the right angle.

"That's a wrap, everyone," Lucas announced after a few minutes. "Thanks. It was worth the wait."

"I'm sorry again," Jessica said as she was helped back on board. "I hope you got what you wanted."

Lucas grinned back. "Absolutely! Take care of yourself."

He headed over to his assistant, who studied the photos on a laptop. The best two would be a late insert into the glossy ball brochures being presented to every guest tomorrow night. Jessica shrugged on a white towelling robe and fastened the belt tightly.

"Excuse me, would you like a drink?"

She turned around. A man with a long black ponytail stood behind her, holding a tray.

"I'm good, thanks."

"Try one," he insisted. "The non-alcoholic fruit punch is delicious."

The waiter's face was heavily lined, and his black eyebrows looked like they'd been plucked. She'd never seen him before, yet his voice was familiar. Staring at his bitten fingernails, she frowned.

"Er, do I know you?"

"Look closely, Jessica," he whispered.

Her mouth fell open. She recognized his grey eyes. "Nathan?"

"Not here." He jerked his head towards the door. "Why don't I show you how I mix the best fresh-mint lemonade you've ever tasted?" he said loudly.

Jessica followed him below deck to a small study.

"In here," he said. "We'll be safe for a few minutes."

She stepped inside. "I can't believe it's you."

Nathan pulled off the rubber mask that encased his head and neck. He scratched his scalp.

"It itches like crazy, but I had to see you. Using MI6's prosthetics department was the only way I could break cover." He gestured for her to sit down. "How are you?"

"OK, I guess, considering." She touched the back of her head. "It doesn't hurt too much now. Thanks for the gadgets, by the way. I'd have been dead without them."

Nathan shuddered. "Let's not even go there. I was wrong to get you caught up in something as risky as this. Jack will kill me if he finds out. This has to stop now."

Jessica studied his face. It was hardened with determination, but no way could he persuade her to back out.

"Dad will kill *me* anyway if he discovers I knew you were out of your coma."

"Touché. But seriously, I can handle this from here on. Your mission to protect Kat is over, and your cover's blown as far as Mr Ingorokva's concerned, so he has no reason to keep you here. Mrs T agrees – you can't stay out here any longer. We're putting you on a flight back to London tonight before you're placed in any more danger."

"No! Please don't do that. Sure, I helped unmask Fake Fed, but I came here to bring Margaret down, and we haven't done that yet."

Nathan cracked his knuckles, making her wince.

"It was never going to be easy to get Margaret, you knew that all along. She covers her tracks well. So does Allegra."

Nathan tossed his mask on the table; the rubber sank into a grotesque face. Jessica ignored the weird features staring up at her. She had to distract him from the whole sending her home business.

"What *do* you have on Allegra?"

"Not much," he admitted. "I pulled satellite images from the night you were attacked, but the pictures are too grainy to give us anything useful. MI6 in London is trawling CCTV footage from around Monaco to try and get a hit on Allegra – or better still Allegra and Margaret together – but so far the facial-recognition technology has drawn a blank."

"Allegra has to be hiding somewhere," Jessica said. "Don't you think Margaret might know where she is? She could be involved with Fake Fed too. They could all be in on this together – hired by an enemy of Mr Ingorokva's to kill Kat and steal the weapon before he has a chance to sell it. It'd be an attack on all fronts – destroying him personally and through his business."

Nathan nodded. "It's a possible scenario. Margaret worked with Allegra in Paris and knows more than she's letting on. But MI6 can't afford to show its hand by bringing her in for questioning. I have to find evidence that ties her once and for all to Allegra – and possibly to the fake Dr Fedorovna."

Jessica winced at the word "I". They both had to come up with the goods to nail Margaret.

"I'm going to have to tell Margaret what's happened to the fake doctor," she said. "If they're working together, she'll realize he's missing before long and will wonder why I didn't mention seeing Mr Ingorokva take him away."

"You're right. You should inform her that Mr Ingorokva's taken the law into his own hands. We don't have a fix on the doctor's location yet, but Mr Ingorokva probably still has him in Monaco." Nathan cracked his knuckles again before Jessica could stop him. "That's if he's still alive, which I very much hope he is."

He shot a pointed look at her.

"I know, I know. I should have waited until I heard back from you, but I was worried for Kat. I didn't want him to get back on board."

Nathan sighed and rubbed his forehead. "You're headstrong, that's for sure. When I'm back in London, we're going to need a little talk about who gives the orders."

Jessica flushed. "I'm sorry. Can't you arrest Mr Ingorokva and ask him what he's done with the doctor?"

"MI6 can't afford to scare him off and blow tomorrow's meeting. We need it to go ahead so we can arrest him and the buyer once the money has changed hands. We also need to seize the weapon. That's the number one priority."

"What do you think it is?"

"You said it's worth 800 million euros, so we're not talking about a gun. It could be chemical, nuclear or even a biological weapon like a vial of smallpox."

Jessica's eyes widened. "He's hiding something like *that* on his yacht? Close to Kat?"

"Mr Ingorokva must believe it's contained, otherwise he'd never risk bringing it on board or taking it to the ball. Whatever it is, I have to get it before anyone else does."

"How are *we* going to stop Mr Ingorokva?"

Nathan shook his head. "I'm going to stop him, not you. I told you – this is over as far as you're concerned."

Yeah, right. "How do you think you're going to get up close and personal to Mr Ingorokva at the ball? That's something only I can do. I can watch him the entire night and see when he makes his move."

"You seem to have forgotten that you'll be back in London," he retorted.

"Not after I burst into tears and beg Mr Ingorokva to let me stay. 'I'm so excited about the ball tomorrow night, and I'll be completely devastated if I have to miss it. I'll be letting down the organizers of the catwalk show, the other models and, of course, Kat. She doesn't know I'm undercover and will expect me to walk the runway with her. How will you explain my sudden absence?' Blah, blah, blah. Did I mention Becky's an aspiring actress? She's given me a few lessons."

Nathan went to crack his knuckles again, but Jessica placed her hand over his. "You know it makes sense to have me there and it's a plausible enough cover story. The catwalk show still has to go ahead. The organizers need me in it – I've had the dress fittings. It'll be too late to get the gowns altered for another model."

He pulled his hand away. "True. This all makes sense from an MI6 perspective, from Mrs T's point of view, to use you rather than a Westwood model as you're already embedded in Mr Ingorokva's entourage. But I'm also your godfather, remember?"

Jessica shrugged. "I don't need you to look after me. I'm a big girl and I can make my own decisions. I want to do this"

"I understand that, but I'm supposed to protect you. If this meet goes horribly wrong and the bomb, or whatever the weapon is, accidentally goes off at the palace..." His voice trailed off.

"Then everyone in Monaco will be slaughtered, including me," Jessica said abruptly. "And if it's a nuclear weapon, I could be killed even if I'm back in

London with Dad. We're in this together. Let's finish this thing while we have the chance."

Nathan drummed his fingers on the table, frowning hard.

God, he was stubborn. What was he waiting for? This was the best option by far. He had to realize that, surely? She'd have Mr Ingorokva eating out of her hand when she stressed how unhappy Kat would be if she missed the catwalk show.

"You know I won't go home willingly," she continued. "You'll have to drag me kicking and screaming back to London, which will alert Margaret and potentially blow *your* cover."

"I get it," he groaned. "You're the most stubborn person I've ever met."

"Determined too."

"How could I forget? God help me when your father finds out."

Great. He was definitely weakening.

"Dad's a pro," she pointed out. "I bet he'd prefer to be a bit miffed about me going behind his back than discovering a nuclear bomb went off and we could have done something to prevent it."

Nathan threw his hands in the air. "I give up. You've got me."

"So what's the plan? *Our* plan?"

"I can't make an arrest inside the palace as it'll cause a major diplomatic incident, but Mrs T's already approved a black ops mission with Westwood, which is being kept off Margaret's radar. I'm using some new model recruits that she doesn't know about." He paused. "I'll have to talk to Mrs T about you being my eyes and ears on the ground. I expect she'll OK it; she's desperate for a result. It'll mean you wearing the diamond earrings with the embedded microphone I gave you. The Westwood girls will back you up if anything goes wrong."

"How will I know who they are?"

"I'll tell them to make eye contact but not to approach you. We don't know who'll be watching tomorrow night. They'll be miked up too, but will only come on board if you need help. As soon as you see Mr Ingorokva heading to the meet, you'll need to follow him, get a visual on the buyer and alert me."

"Then what?"

"We'll swoop as soon as the buyer leaves the palace.

Once they're arrested we'll pick up Mr Ingorokva too."

"It's risky," Jessica said. "What if you don't catch the buyer on the way out?"

"We will. They have no reason to suspect we're on to them. If they're brazen enough to turn up to the Grimaldi Ball, they'll be doing it by invitation only. They must be planning to walk in and out the main entrance, along with the other guests; it's a far safer plan than risking getting caught by security scaling the walls or breaking in via another door."

"What about Mr Ingorokva?"

"If he tries to run, he won't get very far," Nathan said. "We'll impound his private jet and yacht."

"It sounds like you've got everything covered. Let's hope we don't get thrown a curve ball."

"You never know, which means you mustn't take any unnecessary risks. That's an order. If you can't get a good enough look at the buyer without exposing yourself, back off and I'll direct a Westwood model to move in and replace you. We're photographing everyone entering the palace, so anyone carrying a briefcase will be flagged and tailed after they exit."

"What about Margaret? Do I tell her about the meet?"

"No," Nathan said slowly. "I'm guessing Margaret knows already. She's probably bugged Mr Ingorokva's phones to keep tabs on his movements and will have overheard the conversation, like you. There's no point alerting her that you're on to the plot. Just make sure you play up the angle about not wanting to miss the catwalk show, which is why you're staying on in Monaco."

Jessica nodded. "Margaret might finally show her hand. Allegra Knight too."

"Let's hope so," he replied. "It can't be a coincidence that criminals are gathering in Monaco for the century's biggest arms deal."

Nathan left the study first, wearing his prosthetic mask, and headed to the kitchen to keep up his waiter cover. Jessica returned to the changing area, removed her make-up and pulled on a pair of white jeans and blue T-shirt. Walking out, she checked her mobile. A text from Mattie had arrived an hour ago.

Father doing better. Waiting for latest round of tests then coming to Monaco.

What? This was all she needed. Mattie *and* a weapon of mass destruction together in one city. That definitely had the makings of a nuclear war.

Everything OK, Jessica messaged back quickly. *No need to visit :)*

Checking flights. Don't try and stop me. Will text with flight details. Mattie.

There was absolutely no point messaging back; nothing could deter Mattie once she put her mind to something. She just had to hope that her arrival didn't clash with the meet tomorrow night.

She pushed her sunglasses on and said her goodbyes to the shoot's team. The harbour side was busy as usual, with tourists gawping at the super yachts. A few multi-millionaire owners sunned themselves on deck, enjoying the stares. Up ahead, Jessica spotted Margaret across the street, talking to someone in a taxi. She had to get a closer look. She dodged traffic and ran to the other side as Margaret climbed into the taxi. Pulling off the face of her Rolex, she held the telescopic lens up to her eye. She could see the back of a woman's straw summer hat.

Turn around!

She had to see who Margaret was meeting. The hat shifted as the woman glanced out the back window. Jessica gasped as the taxi pulled away. She'd only caught a quick glimpse of her face but could have sworn it was Kat's newly unemployed tutor.

What did Margaret want with Darya?

CHAPTER

SEVENTEEN

Jessica smoothed her shimmering, silver sequined Chanel gown. The scent of flowers filled the air as they travelled to the ball by horse-drawn carriage. Mr Ingorokva had totally bought her story about wanting to stay on in Monaco because she couldn't bear missing this once-in-a-lifetime experience. Plus, she was right – he hadn't wanted to face uncomfortable questions from Kat about her sudden disappearance.

The Grimaldi Palace sparkled like a fairy-tale castle in the distance, illuminated by thousands of lights. She'd feel like Cinderella if Mr Ingorokva weren't sat opposite, scowling and clutching a small briefcase tightly to his chest. Inside was a weapon of mass destruction. Something deadly, but valuable enough to be worth Allegra and Margaret both breaking cover for. What if he accidentally dropped the briefcase and released whatever was inside? They'd die. Everyone in Monaco would be wiped out.

The smell of flowers was suffocating. She gripped the carriage door as panic ballooned in her chest. Her hand crept towards the handle.

"Are you all right?" Mr Ingorokva leant forwards, still hugging his briefcase. "You look a little pale."

"I'm fine, thanks." Jessica's voice sounded small and tinny. Her hand dropped to her lap. "Apart from being a bag of nerves about the show."

"Well you'd better not mess up," Kat said sullenly. "I don't want you to make me look bad." She was a vision in her gold, embroidered Elie Saab dress, which had a massive train. It was from the designer's bridal collection, but Kat had insisted upon wearing it because it showed off her new ruby earrings. She had matching fingerless gold-lace gloves to cover up the wound on her hand.

Jessica looked away. She could feel Mr Ingorokva's eyes burning into her face. Had he guessed she was on to him? What would he do if he found out? He'd probably shoot her. She returned his gaze. She'd fight to the death if it came to it. Whatever happened tonight, she couldn't let him go through with this deal. There was too much at stake.

Kat hung over the side of the carriage and gazed at the palace. "It's so beautiful. Do you think they lit it up especially for me?"

She didn't pause for breath as Jessica and Mr Ingorokva remained silent.

"I've always wanted my own castle. How much do they cost? Do you think you'll ever buy one, Papa?"

Mr Ingorokva grunted, which was enough to satisfy Kat as she chattered excitedly. Jessica sank back into her seat and surreptitiously wiped her damp palms on the red velvet seat. A bead of sweat dropped from Mr Ingorokva's brow. He was feeling the pressure too. No wonder. He was about to conduct a deadly multi-million arms deal. If it went wrong, everyone in the palace – including his daughter – could die.

"Look! Everyone's staring at us!" Kat exclaimed. "They must be waiting to catch a glimpse of me."

She gave a regal wave to the throng of tourists that had congregated outside the palace walls.

"I think they're probably more interested in seeing the Royal Family," Jessica pointed out.

Kat ignored her and continued to wave and throw kisses.

The carriage passed through the gates and was directed into the courtyard by a man dressed from head to toe in white. Jessica climbed down carefully, determined not to trip and fall in front of the gathered photographers. Her mouth fell open as they were escorted into the palace. It might be the height of summer but the palace had been transformed into a Russian winter wonderland, with sumptuous furnishings, fairy-tale lights and giant ice sculptures of swans. Staff dressed in elaborate red-and-gold costumes and masks lined up to offer refreshments.

"It's amazing," Kat squealed. She swished her skirts and straightened her veil.

"I'm glad you appreciate it," her father said briskly. "Tonight's cost me a fortune."

Jessica stared straight ahead. Who was he kidding?

He wasn't doing Kat any favours. This was all about his arms deal and nothing else.

"This is a very important night for me." Mr Ingorokva stopped and fiddled with his bow tie.

"Let me do it, Papa." Kat retied the bow perfectly and tweaked it into place.

He pulled away, exasperated. "Enough, already. I expect you both to behave yourselves and not to embarrass me in any way. Do not touch the vodka or champagne and do not go into the restricted areas. The Royal Family's quarters are strictly off-limits for guests. Do you understand?"

Kat flinched at his harsh tone. Jessica nodded. She had every intention of trailing Mr Ingorokva and his mystery contact into the off-limit areas. She had a sneaking suspicion that Kat was itching to explore the palace too.

A waiter approached carrying a large silver tray. "Champagne, sir?"

"Not now." Mr Ingorokva caught sight of someone across the foyer and stalked away. Had he spotted the person he'd arrange to meet? Jessica walked after him but Kat grabbed her arm.

"Have you seen these ice sculptures? I must find out who created them. I'd love to have some made up back home."

"Yes, you should go and find out."

And leave me alone tonight, Jessica wanted to add.

She tried to walk away but Kat held her arm tight.

"I'm so stupid. I forgot mama's diamond bracelet. I can't do the show without it. Papa's expecting me to wear it."

"He probably won't even notice." Mr Ingorokva had bigger things on his mind tonight than his daughter's jewellery.

"You don't understand. It's a good-luck charm. I wear it when I'm nervous to remind me of mama. It gives me confidence. I have to wear it."

Wow. Kat really did have a soft side. Jessica usually wore *her* mum's necklace all the time. Nathan's life-saving pendant still felt odd around her neck. She'd dispensed with it for the first time tonight as Kat had insisted on loaning her a platinum diamond necklace. She wasn't planning to go close to water anyway.

"I understand where you're coming from," Jessica

said, gently. "But there isn't time to go back to the yacht."

"Sure there is." Kat waved her hand dismissively. "I left it on the dressing table in my cabin. I'll ring ahead and make sure security let you back on board."

So much for Kat having a soft side. "This might sound like a silly question, but why don't *you* go back?"

Kat tapped her gold Christian Louboutin foot impatiently. "Papa expects me to mingle and meet important guests, but no one's going to miss you. You'll only be gone half an hour. What's the problem?"

"I could miss the start of the show."

Yeah, that was a lame excuse, but what if Mr Ingorokva brought forward the meet? She couldn't afford to miss seeing the buyer. "Sorry, I don't want to risk it. Why don't you ask a bodyguard to get it?"

Kat's eyes narrowed. "They're useless. You'll be back in plenty time if you leave now. You're much quicker at getting ready than me anyway."

"No, thanks."

"Didn't I make myself clear?" Her face hardened. "I'm not asking you to get it, I'm telling you. If you say no again, I'll tell Papa that you're planning to explore the restricted areas."

"What?"

"Don't bother denying it. I saw the look on your face when Papa warned us to stay away. What are you planning to do? Steal the royal jewels?"

"Of course not, I—"

"You owe me, anyway, remember? I saved your life."

"Do as she says," Nathan whispered to Jessica through the diamond-earring communicator inside her ear. "You've got time. We can't let the brat scupper tonight."

Jessica glared at Kat. She wasn't aware she'd betrayed any emotion when Mr Ingorokva talked about the off-limit areas. She needed to be more careful around her; she didn't miss a trick. Taking a deep breath, she stretched out her hand. "Key card?"

Kat retrieved it from her Armani clutch bag. "Hurry now. I don't want you to embarrass Papa by being late for my show."

She swept away into the ballroom, her glittering train swishing behind her.

"Unbelievable," Jessica said through gritted teeth.

"Agreed," said Nathan.

The horse-drawn carriages looked glamorous, but they took for ever. Jessica hopped in a taxi and managed to get back on board *Lilya* within twenty minutes. She'd never been inside Kat's cabin before. It looked as though a bomb had gone off. Either Kat had been robbed or she was having yet another wardrobe clear-out. Designer dresses were strewn across the floor. A ruby Jimmy Choo sandal lay on the bed along with a brown apple core and a broken Louis Vuitton clutch.

Jessica stepped over the gowns and searched the dressing table, along with the contents of a jewellery box. *Typical*, she fumed. There were plenty of diamond earrings and necklaces but no diamond bracelets. She tried calling Kat's mobile but it went straight to voicemail. Where was her blasted bracelet? Did Kat even know?

Nathan came back on the comms. "You need to get a move on. Westwood's reported that Mr Ingorokva's getting twitchy and repeatedly checking his watch."

Jessica touched her ear. "I'm on it."

She tried the top drawer and stopped. What? How dare Kat? She pulled out *her* sunglasses, the gift from her dad. Kat must have nicked them after she'd left them on the jet and blamed the cleaners. She had some nerve. She probably had no intention of giving them back; they were another little trinket that *happened* to fall into her handbag.

Jessica clicked on the thermal-imaging function. The glasses still worked. Hopefully, Kat hadn't discovered *that* while she'd been admiring herself in the mirror for the zillionth time.

She glanced at Kat's gold Cartier bedside clock. The models would already be in make-up backstage. Checking under the bed, she discovered a plate of half-eaten toast and several Chanel nail polishes but no bracelet. How would she ever find it? Kat must have left it in a silly place, like the pocket of one of her jackets. This was when her dad's sunglasses could prove useful. Tapping on the lens, she activated the menu and switched the thermal-imaging function over to X-ray. It was the same technology used in airports, so it'd flag up any metal objects, including the gold and platinum settings of jewellery.

Now she'd see exactly how many jewels Kat possessed. Probably millions.

First, she scanned the walk-in wardrobe, flicking through her outfits one by one. Nothing. No random jewels left in pockets. Next she turned her attention to her shoeboxes. They all had photos of designer stilettos and sandals stuck to them. Normal people didn't leave a diamond bracelet lying around in a shoebox, but she wouldn't put it past Kat. She had to look in the least obvious places. As she moved a pile of boxes out of the way, something under the wardrobe lit up.

The glasses had detected metal beneath the cream carpet; a hole containing strangely shaped objects. Jessica pulled the carpet back. Kat had a hidden safe. If her mum's bracelet was as precious as she claimed it was, maybe she'd actually been sensible and locked it inside. She grabbed her sequin Stella McCartney clutch bag and fished out her diamanté key ring. Scanning it across the keyboard, it detected fingerprints on four numbers – 9, 5, 4 and 1. Jessica placed the key ring on the safe and waited as the mini-computer cracked the number order.

The light turned green and she pulled the lever. The inside was stuffed with cheap plastic bags and bundles of paper instead of the Tiffany jewellery boxes she'd been expecting. Jessica pulled out a pile of newspaper cuttings. They were all about various thefts, including Madison Matthews' Oscar necklace and the ornament from the Frick Collection. Kat had also kept the newspaper article about this week's burglary at the Hermitage Hotel in Monaco.

Why was she so interested in this sort of stuff?

"Have you found it yet?" Nathan's voice crackled in her ear.

"Give me a minute. I've got into the safe."

Jessica heaved out a bulky plastic bag, which contained a slightly chipped vase. It looked familiar. It couldn't be. She snatched up the newspaper article about the Frick theft and stared at the photo of the missing ornament.

"Ohmigod!" She was holding the stolen porcelain. Why was it in Kat's safe?

She grabbed another bag and pulled out a handful of rose-coloured diamonds. Studying the pic of Madison Matthews, her heart pounded.

"No way!" They were an exact match to the singer's stolen necklace.

"What's going on?" Nathan demanded.

She ignored him and pulled out more bags. They were packed with jewels. The emerald necklace and sapphire bracelet fitted the description of jewellery stolen from the Hermitage Hotel by the cat burglar.

She sat back on her heels, dazed.

"Are you still with me?" Nathan said urgently. "Give me an update. What's happening?"

"Er, nothing. I'm kind of blown away by Kat's jewellery collection."

Something told her to delay disclosing her discovery to Nathan, at least until after she'd confronted Kat. Even though Kat was a total nightmare, she owed her the chance to explain. Nathan could have her arrested.

"For God's sake, focus!" Nathan yelled.

Jessica clamped her hand to her ear. "OW!"

"You don't have time for window shopping. Get back to the ball. That's an order."

Using her Swarovski compact, she quickly scanned the ornament and some of the jewels for fingerprints. Yes! There were prints on the porcelain, sapphire bracelet and Madison Matthews' necklace. Pressing the central gem, she took a photo of each print. She could upload them to the MI6 database later.

"Leaving now. I've got it."

She leapt up, shoving her sunglasses into her clutch bag. Kat was storing millions of pounds worth of stolen jewellery in her cabin. How had she got hold of it? Either she'd swiped everything herself or was hiding the stash for someone else. Whatever the truth, Kat was in a stack of trouble. Jessica doubted whether even Mr Ingorokva would be able to buy her way out of this almighty mess.

CHAPTER
EIGHTEEN

Getting back into the Grimaldi Palace took twenty minutes of wrangling with the security guards; Jessica had accidentally left her invitation and wristband in the carriage. Becoming hopelessly lost inside the palace wasted another ten minutes. Now she was horribly late. She bombed into the changing room, where stylists were putting the final touches to the models' looks.

Kat was resplendent in ruby lace Dolce & Gabbana. If Jessica wasn't very much mistaken, it was the dress *she* was supposed to be wearing.

"Careful you don't ruin my hair," Kat ordered as a woman placed a glittering jewel-studded gold crown on her head. She glanced up at Jessica.

"There you are, finally! I didn't think you were coming back so I figured I should wear your dress. It was a shame to waste it. Give me my bracelet." She clicked her fingers and stretched out her hand.

Jessica walked over and dropped a glittering trinket in her palm.

"What's this? It's not mine, you idiot." Kat squinted at the bracelet. "I said diamonds, not sapphires."

Jessica fiddled with her earring, turning off the microphone so Nathan couldn't hear. She snatched the bracelet back and slipped it into her clutch bag.

"I know this doesn't belong to you," she whispered in her ear. "It's from the Hermitage Hotel raid. The vase from the Frick museum and Madison Matthews' necklace don't belong to you either. What are they doing in your safe?"

Kat's jaw dropped. Her face paled. "I don't ... I don't know what you're talking about."

"Yes, you do. I think—"

"*Zut alors*! You are très, *très en retard*," a voice shrieked.

A woman grabbed Jessica and bundled her into the corner before she could interrogate Kat further. Stylists pounced, helping her into a strapless, emerald-green Dior gown. A make-up artist and hairstylist got to work with an array of brushes, grips and eyeshadow palettes.

She could feel Kat's eyes burning into her as they created her look; a modern-day Rapunzel with a red wig. The tresses wound into a long plait, which trailed along the floor. She longed to rip off the heavy hairpiece. It pressed down on to her scalp, rubbing against the stitches.

A Rihanna track blared out as the models were herded towards the door.

"This is it, people," the stage manager shouted. "The order is – Kat, Jessica, Tania, Lisbeth, Sabby, Olive, Juanita and Rizzola. Move it, girls! We haven't got all day." He clapped his hands impatiently.

"Ouch!" Jessica's wig was almost torn from her scalp as a model accidentally stepped on her plait. A few grips fell to the floor.

"Whoops! Sorry!" The redhead flashed a smile as she shuffled into line. Jessica stared at her large opal earrings. Did they contain microphones? She could be Westwood. She'd definitely made eye contact. She'd held her gaze a few seconds longer than necessary.

Kat fidgeted with her dress as Jessica hauled herself into place behind her. "We need to talk," Kat began.

"And three, two, one, go," the stage manager announced. "Now!"

Kat stumbled slightly as she emerged to claps and cheers. Jessica watched from the wings as she waited to be counted in next. Kat didn't have her usual swagger down the catwalk. She looked as if she were struggling to keep upright in her killer silver heels. Posing quickly for the photographers, she turned and stalked back.

"Go, Jessica!" the stage manager cried.

She took her time as she sashayed towards Kat. If she tried to rush, she'd trip over her wig and fall flat on her face; that wasn't a shot she wanted her classmates back home to see. Kat shot her a pleading look as they passed.

"Please don't say a word to Papa," she whispered.

They parted again. Lights exploded in Jessica's face as she reached the end of the catwalk, thrust out her hips and curved her back. This was the money shot; the picture that all the photographers wanted, as it would be used by magazines across the world. It could make or break a model. She knew she'd nailed it.

Her eyes drifted across the audience. A woman in a

royal-blue evening gown sat in the front row, watching her intently. Jessica struck another pose, brushing her hand against her earring. She turned the mic back on again. "Margaret's here," she said under her breath. "As we suspected."

"Keep calm," Nathan said in her earpiece. "Your priority is getting a visual on the buyer. We'll deal with Margaret if she makes a move."

She turned and walked back up the catwalk. A blonde model stared with piercing blue eyes as she passed. This must be the other undercover model from Westwood. It was reassuring to know she had backup.

Backstage, assistants immediately jumped on her, stripping off the jewels and gown before she had a chance to catch her breath. They helped her into a stunning feather-and-sequin white Armani Privé dress with a heavily embroidered silver stole. Kat was already in her second outfit – a sumptuous purple Valentino corseted number. Her face was ashen beneath the powder as a woman touched up her make-up.

"So are you going to tell me what's going on?" Jessica said quietly.

Kat batted away the make-up artist. "How did you

get into my safe, anyway? The combination's secret. I could probably get you arrested for breaking and entering."

"You ordered me back to your cabin to look for your bracelet, remember? I didn't want to be there. I stumbled across the safe and guessed the combination. Anyway, I wouldn't start threatening me with the police if I were you. You're the one who's been handling stolen property."

Kat burst into tears. "Please don't say that. I don't know what to do. You have to help me. I think I've been really dumb."

Jessica grabbed a box of tissues and handed her one. "What have you done exactly? I can't help you unless you tell me the truth."

Kat dabbed at the mascara pouring down her powdered cheeks. "I never use the safe. It drives Papa mad; you know how I never put anything away and am always losing things."

Jessica nodded. "He wanted you to put the Fabergé egg in his safe, but you refused."

"So you have to believe me, I had no idea all that stolen gear was in there."

"The jewellery didn't hop in on its own."

Kat took a deep breath, twisting the tissue around her finger. "A friend said he had some birthday presents for his mother and wanted to keep them locked up. He didn't want to ask Papa so I offered my safe as a favour. I didn't think it'd be a problem. I gave him a spare key card to my room and the safe's combination. I didn't think anything more about it until today. I never checked what was inside."

Jessica groaned. "By any remote chance, is your friend Dr Fedorovna or whatever he's calling himself now?"

"Of course," Kat said, sniffing. "You must have realized by now that I'd do absolutely anything for Andrei."

Jessica rolled her eyes. How could she have been so stupid?

"What's going to happen to me? Are you going to tell the police?" Kat dabbed her eyes. "Please help me. I can't go to prison. It'd destroy Papa. I'm all he's got."

"Whatever's going on with Kat, you need to wrap it up right now," Nathan barked in her ear.

Jessica jumped guiltily. She'd forgotten to switch

off the microphone. Nathan had heard every word. So much for keeping her lawbreaking a secret.

"I don't care about any of this," he insisted. "A Westwood agent's seen Mr Ingorokva leaving the audience. The meet must have been brought forward. Go after him."

"Don't worry," Jessica said, squeezing her shoulder. "I'll help you deal with this."

Kat caught her hand. "Do you promise? Are you going to tell anyone what you saw? Because if you do, I'll be in so much trouble."

"We'll talk about this later. I have to go." She broke free and pushed her way through the stylists.

"Where are you going?" Kat shouted after her. "We're on right now!"

The stage manager glanced up from his clipboard. "Come back!" he yelled. "You've got thirty seconds. There's no time for a toilet break."

Jessica ignored them. She grabbed her mobile and stuffed it into her gown pocket as she fled the room. She kicked off her crystal-studded stilettos and doubled back to the main corridor in bare feet, just in time to see Mr Ingorokva stride across the entrance hall. She peered around the corner as he reached the staircase. He ducked under the cordon and entered the restricted area, taking the steps two at a time. Within seconds, he'd disappeared.

She followed up the stairs, careful not to trip on the hem of her dress. Mr Ingorokva was at the end of the corridor. His hand reached for a door handle. She slammed against the wall as he looked over his shoulder. When she peered out again, he'd gone. He must have entered the room.

"Mr Ingorokva's in a room on the first floor," she said softly. "Trying to get a visual now." She ran towards the door straight ahead.

Nathan's voice was in her ear again. "Be careful."

She'd almost reached the door when footsteps pounded towards her. She had to move fast, but Mr Ingorokva could be right behind the door, so she couldn't just barge in. But if she didn't get off the landing, she'd come face-to-face with a security guard or even Mr Ingorokva's mystery contact. She grabbed the door handle of the next room along and slipped inside. *Phew*. The footsteps passed by. She was in a very grand library, lined with books and tables.

Behind a heavy red-velvet curtain, she spotted a set of adjoining doors to the next room. Was Mr Ingorokva in there? Pulling out her compact, she flipped open the X-ray vision lid and stared through the door. Two figures were illuminated on the far side of the room. Carefully, she opened the door a fraction of an inch. She pulled out the listening and visual probe which was embedded in the lining of her Stella McCartney evening bag and poked it through the gap. A black-and-white image flashed up on the mirror inside the clutch. A figure clad in a long cloak stood with her back to Jessica. Skirts peeped out from the hem. Under her breath, she relayed the information to Nathan; they were on the lookout for a woman, about five-feet-nine-tall. She had something in her left hand that Jessica couldn't make out: a tape recorder or some other gizmo?

"Who are you? Was a mask necessary?" Mr Ingorokva stepped into view, speaking English. He fiddled with his bow tie. "I always like to see who I'm doing business with."

"I'm your contact tonight," the woman said, speaking into the device in her hand. "That's all you need to know."

"A voice disguiser too?"

"*Mais oui.* Have you brought it?"

"Of course." Mr Ingorokva walked over to the desk. The woman followed. If only she'd turn around, Jessica could give a description of her mask and physique to Nathan. It could be Allegra; the height was about right but she couldn't tell for sure.

Mr Ingorokva fumbled with the lock of his briefcase for a few seconds before the lid sprang open. Jessica squinted to try and make out what was inside, but the picture quality was too fuzzy. She couldn't see without opening the door wider and blowing her cover.

The woman groped around inside the case.

"It's not here." She grabbed a letter knife from the table and slit open the lining, ripping it apart. Picking up a small piece of card, she held it up to the light. "Is this an Emperor's New Clothes joke that I'm not getting? You think I'm interested in a clothes tag belonging to Kat?" She dropped it on the desk and hurled the briefcase across the room.

"I never joke when it involves 800 million euros," Mr Ingorokva said. "I brought it with me tonight. It's here, in the palace."

"But not in this room?"

"That's correct. Consider it my insurance policy. Transfer the money and I'll give you the location. It's not far from here."

"That wasn't the deal."

"It's the deal now. Take it or leave it. I could always stick to my original plan: sell it to the President and take MI6's cash for stopping the ballot rigging. Your coup will fail and he'll use the weapon to kill every single member of your party. You'd better start running now, lady."

"Are you picking this up?" Jessica whispered to Nathan. "Mr Ingorokva double-crossed MI6. He's doing business with Georgia's opposition party."

"Yes," Nathan said tersely. "Pull out."

"No. I haven't seen her face yet."

"It's too dangerous. We've found a woman's body near the palace. She has links to the Georgian opposition party. We think she was Mr Ingorokva's contact tonight. We've no idea who's with him right now, but it's not whoever he was supposed to be meeting."

"I'm staying a little longer," she replied. "We need to find out where Mr Ingorokva's hidden the weapon."

The woman retrieved an iPad from her cloak. "The money's ready to be transferred to your bank account as we agreed." She switched the device on and appeared to navigate to a page. "You need to enter your account number here." She pointed to the screen.

Mr Ingorokva bent over the desk and tapped in a number.

"The transaction's being completed right now," Jessica said softly.

A loud *crack* rang out. Mr Ingorokva fell backwards, clutching his chest. Jessica caught her breath. The woman's hand was steady as she pointed the gun at his head.

"Mr Ingorokva's down!" Jessica hissed. "He's been shot."

"This is the new deal," she continued. "I don't play games. Tell me where it is right now."

"You can't kill me," Mr Ingorokva gasped. "You'll never find it without me. It's impossible."

"But I can, with your daughter's help." She picked up the phone, which had fallen out of his jacket pocket. "Let's ring Kat and ask her to join our little party. I have the feeling you'll be more cooperative with her around."

"No! Leave Katyenka alone."

The woman dialled and spoke into her voice disguiser again. "Hello? Is that Kat? I'm a friend of your father's—"

"I'll tell you," he panted. "I promise you I'll tell you. Hang up."

"Your father's in the first-floor drawing room and needs to see you right away." His assailant threw the phone down. "You've got approximately four minutes before your daughter arrives and I kill her, so start talking."

"The location was written in the briefcase. You held it in your hands a moment ago."

"What?" She darted across the room to the briefcase. She held it upside down and shook it before feeling beneath the lining again.

Jessica's eyes widened. Did Mr Ingorokva mean the clothes tag? He could have written some kind of code on the card. She pushed the door open a little wider. Through the crack, she could see the tag lying next to a writing pad and pot of gold fountain pens on the desk.

It looked like the ones that had been attached to her gowns before the show. She could get to it. She had to get to it.

The woman spun around, revealing a Venetian mask. She must have spotted the tag too. She launched herself at the desk. Jessica flew through the door and got there first. She snatched it up and kicked her attacker in the stomach. The figure wheezed, dropping the gun and the voice disguiser. Jessica followed it up by a kick to the chin, which sent her sprawling across the room.

The woman picked herself up again and propelled herself at Jessica.

CRACK!

The gun discharged again. The woman screamed, gripping her shoulder as she fell backwards. Her mask fell off.

Darya stared down at her hands, which dripped with blood.

CHAPTER
NINETEEN

Mr Ingorokva's hand wavered as he held the gun. He said something in Russian, and Jessica squeezed the butterfly behind her earring, which instantly translated his words.

"Why are you doing this?"

"Why do you think?" Darya snarled back, also in Russian. She moved towards the door.

"Money," breathed Mr Ingorokva. "Of course."

"You would think that, but I'm more interested in power. That's a far more valuable commodity to me."

Mr Ingorokva shook his head in disbelief as she continued.

"You should be more careful about who you do business with. Word leaked out about the weapon's existence months ago. I'm only surprised that more interested parties didn't turn up to claim it tonight."

"It was a risk. I always knew that." Mr Ingorokva's breathing sounded laboured. "But no one else dared to violate the rules of business. You came aboard my yacht. You took advantage of my hospitality and got close to Katyenka as the doctor did. You'll both pay for that. I'll see to that eventually."

"Will you? You have the best security money can buy, yet the doctor managed to escape from right under your nose. That was extremely careless."

"No doubt you played a part in breaking him out of my warehouse. My guards are still recovering from your gas attack."

Darya smirked. "You were sloppy. You thought no one would come looking for the doctor. But I have to admit you hid the weapon well. I'll give you that. Neither of us could locate it on board *Lilya*."

"You both crossed a line." Mr Ingorokva clasped both hands around the weapon as Darya backed away. "Stay where you are."

"Even you wouldn't kill someone in cold blood. Look around you. None of your hired thugs are here to do your dirty work for you. Just a teenage girl." She shot a withering look in Jessica's direction. "Another loose end we should have finished off while we had the chance."

Jessica blinked. Her words were strangely familiar, even in Russian.

"Don't even think of coming after me, Jessica," she hissed in English. "Or my colleague will kill you."

Darya staggered to the door, leaving behind a trail of blood. She gave a searing last look at Jessica and vanished.

"Did you get all that, Nathan? Darya has a gunshot wound and is on the move but doesn't know the weapon's location," she said, running over to Mr Ingorokva. "We need an ambulance urgently."

"It's on the way. Stay where you are. We'll pick up Darya," Nathan instructed. "We're moving in right now."

Jessica tugged at Mr Ingorokva's dinner jacket, revealing a small hole in his white shirt where the bullet had entered. She ripped it open, exposing a protective vest.

"Hurts to breathe," he wheezed. "Katyenka."

237

"Don't worry. Darya won't be able to get to her."

Mr Ingorokva's head lolled to one side as he passed out.

Jessica felt his wrist. His pulse was weak. She'd done enough first-aid training at school to know that she had to loosen his bow tie and start CPR. She pumped his chest, counting the beats in her head. Once he started breathing more easily, she put him in the recovery position and sat back on her heels.

"His vest took the bullet but he's unconscious," she told Nathan urgently. "How long before help gets here?"

"The ambulance is outside the palace. Paramedics will be with you in minutes," he reported back into her earpiece.

The door banged open and Kat flew in, her ethereal blue gown flowing. Margaret and two security guards joined her.

"Papa!" she cried, falling to her knees by his side. "What happened?"

"He's been shot," Jessica explained. "Paramedics will be here shortly. Luckily, he was wearing a bulletproof vest, but he's having difficulty breathing."

Kat's mouth fell open. "Shot? Ohmigod. Papa!"

She shook her father's shoulders but he remained unconscious. "Who did this to him?" she sobbed.

"It was Darya," Jessica replied. "She didn't know about the vest."

Kat flinched. "My old tutor? That can't be right. I don't believe you."

"I saw her do it. It was definitely Darya."

"Why would she do that?"

"I have no idea," Jessica lied.

"This is my fault," Kat wailed. "Darya must have wanted revenge because I got her sacked." She kissed her dad's forehead. "I'm so sorry, Papa. I didn't mean to get you hurt. I planted the Fabergé egg in her wardrobe because I couldn't stand her. I didn't expect her to come back and hurt you like this."

Jessica's eyes widened. She'd been right about Kat setting Darya up.

"This isn't your fault, I promise you." Margaret turned to face Jessica as she stood up. "Fill me in on everything."

"It happened so quickly I didn't have time to alert you. I heard Mr Ingorokva arguing and came in. They each fired off a shot, and Darya was hit in the shoulder. I don't know how badly she's hurt, but she's left a trail."

She pointed to the blood spatter leading to the side door.

"It was lucky you were here to help," Margaret said calmly. "Do you know what they were arguing about?"

Jessica didn't miss a beat. "Darya wanted something. I'm not sure what exactly but I know she didn't get it. That's why she shot him."

Margaret glanced around the room and spotted the briefcase on the floor. "Search the building," she instructed the guards. "Darya can't have got far."

They peeled away, speaking urgently into their earpieces.

"Go with them," Margaret told Jessica. "I'll wait with Mr Ingorokva and Kat for the paramedics."

"Of course."

Margaret wanted to get rid of her so she could search Mr Ingorokva's briefcase. But she wouldn't find the clue. Jessica had already stuffed the clothes tag into the pocket of her gown. Margaret wouldn't be getting anything out of Mr Ingorokva either in his current state.

She passed the paramedics as she pelted down the corridor, following the blood trail down the stairs. She spotted smears on the entrance-hall floor. Someone had walked through the blood without realizing it.

"Darya must be heading out the front gate," Jessica said quietly. "I think I know where Mr Ingorokva's hidden the weapon. I'm going for it now."

"Wait—" Nathan began.

Jessica winced as static buzzed in her ears.

"I want—" His words were muffled by interference again. "Where—? I'm coming in."

"I can't hear you properly, Nathan. I'm going backstage. I'll check in with you in five."

Jessica ran towards the changing area. The show had finished and the models were back in their "civvie" gear, scrubbing off their theatrical make-up with cotton-wool balls.

The stage manager turned beetroot as she burst in. "What happened to you?" he shrieked.

"There was an emergency upstairs. I had to call an ambulance."

"Haven't you ever heard the saying 'the show must go on'? You ruined my line-up and my dress!" He stared at her torn gown in horror. "I'll never book you again."

"I'm sorry!"

Jessica caught the arm of a young, female stylist as he stalked off.

"What happened to all the gowns?" she said, scanning the room. The rails of designer clothes had vanished.

"They've been packed up and sent off."

"Where?"

"To be dry-cleaned, of course, before they're returned to the designers," she replied. "You wouldn't believe the state of some of them. Why do you want to know, anyway?"

"I think one of my own dresses may have got mixed up with them," Jessica said, thinking on her feet. "I need to get it back before it's taken away."

"Well you'll have to be quick. The whole rail's probably being loaded on to the van as we speak. You'll need to go to the underground service entrance where goods vehicles park."

The stylist reeled off some directions. Jessica broke out into a run. "We can't let the van leave the palace," she said, touching her earpiece. "The weapon has to be among the dresses."

"We'll stop and search each van that leaves," Nathan said. "It's possible Darya's found her way on to one of them. We haven't caught sight of her leaving the main entrance yet."

Using the staff stairs, she made her way deeper inside the palace, towards a vast underground loading area. Caterers were already packing away decorations from tonight's festivities. She spotted a clothing rack, covered in a sheet, next to a large grey van. The doors were wide open but no one was about. She glanced over her shoulder at a sudden commotion. A caterer had dropped a large vase. People scurried about, picking up pieces of glass. They paid no attention to her.

Pulling off the sheet, she ran her fingers along the padded, white silk hangers. The gowns were zipped into long black garment bags to protect them. They were all fastened with the same white tags she'd spotted in Mr Ingorokva's briefcase. Her hunch was

243

right; this had to be where he'd hidden the weapon. But where? She examined the metal rail. It couldn't be large or bulky. It wasn't hidden at the base of the stand. Could it be inside the rail? If so, it would have to be something like a vial of anthrax or smallpox. No way did she want to disturb that by smashing open the metal tube.

First, she'd try the dresses. Mr Ingorokva could have planted something inside the garment bags. The tag was marked KAT, 17. There were eight of them in the show so the tag referred to Kat's third outfit change.

Jessica counted through the dresses. Each had a tag tied to the hanger. She pulled out the seventeenth gown. This was wrong. The tag read COLE, 26. She unzipped the bag. It was one of the dresses she was supposed to wear tonight. Judging by the smear of lipstick on the Vivienne Westwood corset, someone else had been laced into it after she did a runner.

Counting along the rail, she pulled out dress number twenty-six, which was missing a tag. Inside was Kat's pink Elie Saab dress, which looked unworn.

"I don't understand," Jessica said out loud. She

fiddled with her earring. "Can you hear me? There's only a dress inside. No weapon. I repeat, there's no weapon."

Nathan didn't reply. She was probably too far underground to pick up any reception from her microphone. She unzipped each garment bag in turn. The numbers had been mixed up after Kat nabbed some of her dresses.

Had Darya or her accomplice figured out this was where Mr Ingorokva had hidden the weapon and already swiped it? Or was it still hidden here?

Jessica was more methodical this time. She removed the hanger with the missing tag and pulled out the gown. Running her fingers inside the bag, she searched the seams. Nothing had been stitched inside. Reaching to the bottom, her fingers brushed against something cold and snake-like. Hello? What was that? It slipped through her fingers. She peered inside. There was nothing there. How was that even possible?

Staring inside the bag didn't help one little bit. She closed her eyes and felt around. There was something hidden inside, but what? She couldn't tell for sure.

Her fingers touched something satiny. It slid away like sand.

Jessica dived in again. Catching hold of it, she pulled and something landed on her knees. She opened her eyes and looked down. She couldn't see anything below her thighs. It was as if her legs had disappeared.

"What the—?" She scrambled backwards, dropping whatever had landed on her. It was totally weird. Her legs appeared again. She groped around the floor for the strange material and threw it over her arms, which became invisible from the elbow down.

"Unbelievable," she gasped.

She'd read about invisibility cloaks before – but that was sci-fi or wizardry, wasn't it? Yet, she was holding one in her hands – her *invisible* hands. This had to be what Darya was after; what every terrorist in the world was probably after. It was the chance to commit crimes without detection. How many murders would take place if this fell into the wrong hands? An assassin could slip past Secret Service agents in the White House, or strike in Buckingham Palace. They'd never be caught. It'd be a complete mystery how someone had bypassed security and committed the crime.

Was that how the thefts at the Frick museum and the Grammys had happened? But if so, who had used the cloak? It couldn't have been Darya because she'd admitted to Mr Ingorokva that she couldn't find it on board his yacht. But what about Fake Fed? Kat said he'd persuaded her to let him use the safe to store the stolen goods. Had he found the cloak on board the yacht, without telling Darya? He could have pretended he didn't know where it was the night Jessica was attacked. This could have been his insurance policy. He'd have been paid handsomely, along with Darya, to deliver the cloak to their buyer tonight, but did he also have a backup plan? If the meet went bad, he could sell off all the items he'd managed to steal by secretly using it. He knew that Kat worshipped him and would never shop him if she discovered his stash. It must have been worth the risk.

Jessica jumped as a door banged. She looked around. The caterers had vanished. She was totally alone. There was a sudden *click*. She'd heard that noise before. Someone had pulled the safety catch off a gun.

Throwing the cloak over her body, she stumbled as she tried to stand up. She caught hold of the rail,

247

making the hangers swing. To her surprise, she could see perfectly through the cloak even though there weren't any eye holes. How was that even possible? She raised her arms and then her foot. She was totally invisible.

Resting her fingers on the rail, she steadied the gowns, but was too late. Someone had heard the noise. Backing away, a figure stepped out from behind a pillar, holding a gun.

Margaret!

CHAPTER
TWENTY

Jessica held her breath as Margaret aimed the gun directly at her. Could she see through the cloak? She was about to run when Margaret turned around and pointed the gun in the other direction, then to her left and right as she moved slowly towards the clothes rail.

"Is someone here?" Margaret shouted. "You can come out, whoever you are. I won't shoot. I'm with MI6. I'm here to help you. You have to hand over what you've found. It's Government property."

No way could she risk it; Margaret would kill her. Jessica stood, statue-like, as Margaret grabbed the rail and violently rifled through it. Gown after gown was thrown to the floor.

Suddenly, a caterer appeared. Margaret spun round, aiming her gun. "Get out!" she shouted.

Jessica sidled past Margaret towards the door. Spinning round again, Margaret squinted as she moved her head from side to side. What was she doing? It suddenly hit her. The first night on the yacht, Jessica had sensed someone in the cabin with her. She'd spotted a shifting, shimmering shape in the corner of her eye. Margaret was trying to detect movement in her peripheral vision.

Margaret turned her back again and rummaged through the clothes on the floor, searching for the cloak. How had she known where it would be? Margaret wouldn't hesitate to shoot her to get to it. She made it to the door and grabbed the handle.

"I know you've got it, Jessica," Margaret said coldly. "Come out, come out, wherever you are."

Jessica looked back. Margaret held the empty garment bag and clothes tag in one hand. In the other, her gun pointed in one direction and then another as she attempted to locate her.

"It's best that you hand it over now. Before this turns nasty."

Jessica remained completely still.

"If you want to play, it won't end well for you," she continued. She fired a shot across the bay, which ricocheted from a pillar. "You see, I'll obviously be devastated that I accidentally shot dead a teenage girl when I believed I was being attacked by a terrorist. No one will be any the wiser."

As she fired off another shot over Jessica's left shoulder, the door swung open and a security guard appeared, also armed.

"What's going on down here?" he yelled.

"I'm with Her Majesty's Government and I'm under attack," Margaret called back. "Keep that door shut. They could still be down here."

"Of course." He shut the door but Jessica had already slipped past and pounded up the stairs.

"Nathan, come in," she whispered. "Can you hear me?"

"Yes. Where are you? I lost you back there." Static buzzed again.

"I'm making my way back up to the palace from the loading bay. I found the weapon. You won't believe what it is."

The door below her clanged and footsteps clattered up the stairs. They sounded like heels. Margaret had figured out that she'd left.

"Do you still have the weapon?" Nathan asked.

"I'm wearing it. It's an invisibility cloak. Margaret knows I've got it. She's got a gun and she's coming after me."

The static hissed louder. "What's that noise?" Nathan muttered to someone in the background. "Jessica, get to the main entrance and I'll find you. I'm already in the palace."

"I'm on my way. I'm at the top of the stairs."

A bullet whizzed over her head as she flung open the door. "She's shooting at me!"

"Get off the line," he said urgently. "Someone's got into our system. They're listening in."

Jessica tore the earring out and threw it across the floor. That's how Margaret knew she was down in the loading bay, looking for the weapon. She'd hacked into their comms and retraced her steps from the backstage area. A stylist could have given her the same directions.

Running down the corridor, she threw a look over

her shoulder. The door opened. Margaret had almost reached her. Where was she? She was completely lost. The corridors were labyrinth-like, winding this way and that. She didn't have a clue where the main entrance was. Three security guards ran past, but she could hardly ask them for directions.

She ran on, with Margaret in pursuit. A woman in a long, burgundy ballgown swept past, followed by a gorgeous blonde model. She had to be close to the ballroom now. Throwing open the double doors in front of her, she dived into a spectacular winter wonderland again. Huge ice statues glittered as hundreds of people danced. Reindeers were being shepherded around the outskirts of the dance floor.

"Snow! Unbelievable!" A man pointed to the gold ceiling.

"Amazing!" a woman agreed.

Jessica looked up. Fake snow swirled and danced down towards her.

The guests cheered and reached up to catch the flakes. More people piled on to the dance floor. Jessica bumped into an elderly guest, who turned round, confused.

"What was that?" he muttered.

Jessica staggered backwards, staring down at her arms in horror. The snow was settling on her cloak, clearly revealing the outline of her body.

"Stop!"

The crowd parted behind Jessica to reveal Margaret, pointing a gun at her. A smile hovered on her pink lips. She was about to pull the trigger.

"No!" A figure hurtled at Margaret, sending her sprawling.

Her gun skidded across the floor. She scrabbled after it, but a foot kicked it away again. Her face was flushed with anger as she looked up. A waiter in a red dinner jacket stood over her.

"What do you think you're doing?" she yelled. "I'll get you fired for this. I'm an MI6 agent, here on official business."

The fair-haired man reached down and pulled her to her feet. "I'm so sorry," he said with a little bow. "I mistook you for a common criminal who'd sell your own country for a high enough price."

"What did you say?" Margaret's voice trembled with fury.

"You heard me. You probably recognize my voice

too but can't place it."

Margaret gawped as the waiter peeled off his prosthetic mask.

"Nice disguise, Nathan." She struggled to her feet. "It suits you."

"Thanks. I have to say this was exactly the welcome party I expected from you." He jerked his head towards her gun. "You didn't disappoint."

Margaret struggled to compose herself. "But when did you ... I mean ... You're out of your coma. I'm so happy."

"Drop the act," he snarled. "You hacked into the comms tonight and knew I was here. What have you done with Jessica?"

Margaret shrugged her shoulders, her eyes locked on her gun lying nearby.

"I have no idea what you're talking about. Darya shot Mr Ingorokva, and I've been tracking her. I haven't seen Jessica since she left Mr Ingorokva."

Jessica slipped the cloak off and hooked it beneath her voluminous skirts while no one was watching. "I'm here, Nathan." She pushed through the guests. "I'm OK. She didn't hurt me."

Margaret's eyes narrowed. "There you are. Thank God." Her voice sounded concerned but her eyes roamed Jessica's body, searching for the cloak. "I was so worried about you with Darya on the loose, but now we're all reunited. It's just like old times."

"You mean old times like you trying to kill me again?" Jessica demanded. "Like Paris? You were going to shoot me just now."

"That was you? I had no idea."

"Yes you did—"

"Leave it," Nathan interrupted, picking up Margaret's gun. He flashed his ID to the security guards who'd stormed into the room.

Margaret showed her identification too. "It's good to have you back, Nathan, although I'm not sure how you cleared it with Mrs T after everything you've been accused of. Or did you? Is this some kind of rogue black ops mission? Maybe I should have you arrested."

Nathan stepped towards her and leant over her shoulder.

"Try it," he whispered in her ear. "I'd advise you to back off while you still have a chance. I'm with MI6, which is more than I can say for you. This is the last mission you'll ever be involved in after trying to kill Jessica tonight."

Margaret stared coolly at him. "I have no idea what you're talking about. Mr Ingorokva regained consciousness briefly and told me about the cloak. I was doing my job back there, trying to stop it from falling into the wrong hands. I thought it was Darya beneath the cloak. How could I have known anything different?"

"Save it for when you're back in London. You can explain it to Mrs T face to face." He turned to Jessica. "Let's get out of here."

Margaret frowned at Jessica as he steered her away. Had she worked out where she'd hidden it?

"Do you still have the cloak?" he asked through clenched teeth.

"Yes, don't worry. It's on me." Jessica turned her head, about to look over her shoulder.

"Keep going," Nathan instructed.

"But Margaret?"

"She can't shoot us here with so many witnesses about. We're safe."

"But for how long? She knows I've got the cloak, and now she knows you're back too she'll be after us both. You shouldn't have blown your cover like that."

"It won't make any difference," Nathan said. "As soon as Margaret hacked the comms and heard me talking to you, the pretence was over. But she had to find the cloak, even if it meant killing you to get it."

"Is that why she pressed to head up the mission in Monaco? Maybe she arranged the threat against Kat's life in order to get MI6 involved and allow her to get close to Mr Ingorokva. That way she could be on hand to coordinate Darya and Fake Fed's attempts to locate the cloak, and give the order to finally kill Kat?"

Nathan nodded. "The death threats may have been designed as a distraction from their real business. But I wouldn't rule out that Margaret could have a personal motive for wanting Kat dead – maybe as revenge against Mr Ingorokva for something in the past. But she must have found out that Mr Ingorokva was selling the cloak on the black market and decided it was too good an opportunity to miss, especially when she could use the cover of an MI6 operation to recover and sell it herself."

"To Vectra?"

"Maybe."

The pair walked through the main gates, past the horse-drawn carriages.

"Why didn't you have Margaret arrested while you still had the chance?" Jessica said.

"We don't have enough evidence," he replied. "Margaret claims she didn't realize it was you under the cloak. Her story sounds plausible enough, if you don't know what she's really like."

"But can't you give the police the recording from the comms? Margaret definitely knew it was me when she was shooting in the loading bay. I told you I saw her getting into a taxi with Darya. They must be in on this together."

"The comms blanked out the whole time you were underground so we don't have Margaret on record," Nathan said. "Also, we don't have documentary proof of her meeting Darya – just your word for it."

"Isn't that enough?"

"Not for a trial. Margaret's defence could argue you

made it up because you have a long-standing grudge against her. It would be her word against yours. We couldn't allow you to get up in open court and reveal anything about Westwood anyway."

"So we're back to square one: Margaret gets away with it and Darya and Fake Fed are still on the loose, probably holed up with Allegra somewhere, plotting their next move."

"Not exactly square one," Nathan answered. "Thanks to you we've got what everyone wants: the world's first invisibility cloak; the most valuable tool in modern warfare. You might have helped avert World War Three."

Jessica's mobile beeped in the pocket of her ballgown. She checked the text message and groaned. "Oh God. Not quite."

"What do you mean? What's wrong?"

"Mattie's flight lands at six a.m. She's spitting blood. She's guessed I've been lying to her all along about this trip. How am I going to talk my way out of this mess?"

"Let me," said Nathan. "It's time people know I'm back. I'll pick Mattie up from the airport and explain everything before I ring your father. They shouldn't have to find out about my recovery from someone else."

"And the cloak? What will happen to that?"

"I'll speak to Mrs T and arrange for a military pickup. In the meantime, I want you to hide it on Mr Ingorokva's yacht."

"Is that a good idea?" Jessica frowned.

"It's not ideal, but it's our only option. Margaret could have bought off someone in the local police force. We can't risk trusting the cloak to anyone here."

"But how will I be able to fight off Darya and Margaret if they come back for the cloak? Fake Fed and Allegra must have been looking for it the night they attacked me – they could come back too."

"They won't be able to board the yacht, I promise. Mr Ingorokva's entire security brief will be armed and on guard. There won't be a safer place in Monaco tonight. There's no way that Darya, Allegra or the fake doctor will be able to get back on board. Margaret wouldn't dare go near the yacht either, but I'll upload her photo into the facial-recognition software if it makes you feel safer."

It sounded risky but Nathan was right; they couldn't trust anyone in Monaco. There was no way of knowing who Margaret had on her payroll. She had extensive contacts.

"OK. I guess." She touched her stitches. They were starting to hurt again.

"Don't worry. I'll arrange for the Westwood models to backup the security on board. They won't leave your side."

"Will Mr Ingorokva allow that?"

"He's not in any state to argue," Nathan said. "I've had an update from the hospital. He suffered some internal bleeding from a broken breastbone but will pull through. I think we'll find he agrees to all our demands now he's been caught double-crossing MI6 and the president of Georgia."

"And Kat? What will happen to her? She says she was holding all that stuff in the safe for Fake Fed. He must have found Mr Ingorokva's hiding place and used the cloak in the raids as well as to write the death threat on the mirror in my cabin."

"I don't know, but I'm guessing MI6 won't want to draw attention to the cloak's existence. I imagine the items will be quietly returned and Kat will get a slap on the wrist, nothing more."

"She'll be relieved, but don't expect a thank you from her. That's not her style."

Nathan laughed. "So I hear. Try and get some rest and I'll call you first thing."

"You're not going to stay on the yacht too?"

"I need to brief Mrs T and sort out transportation." He squeezed her shoulder. "Try not to worry about Margaret. She knows it's over. She's played all her cards now."

Jessica shivered. What if she hadn't? Margaret was a pro. She usually had a backup plan.

CHAPTER
TWENTY ONE

Jessica lay on her bed, staring at the motion-sensor lipstick. She hadn't slept a wink. How could she? Her hunch about the blonde and redhead models from the show had been correct; they were Westwood agents called Amber and Helena. They were in cabins further down the corridor. But even their presence – and the fact they were both armed – hadn't reassured her. Neither had the armed guards outside her door. What she'd learnt through her dealings with MI6 so far was scarily simple: if someone really wanted to get to you, they could.

Checking her watch, she prayed that Mattie wouldn't erupt like a volcano when Nathan came clean. Her flight should have landed by now and they'd probably be at the yacht within an hour. It was strange that Nathan hadn't rung already to give her details about the cloak's collection. It must be after his airport run.

She jumped off the bed and peered inside her wardrobe. She'd hung the cloak on a hanger, underneath a heavily embroidered, gold Christian Lacroix evening gown. It had been as good a hiding place as any other.

After a quick shower, she pulled on a pair of skinny jeans, white T-shirt and trainers. She carefully placed the invisibility cloak into her Louis Vuitton holdall and sat with it on her knees.

Come on, Nathan. Don't leave me dangling here. Call me.

Now what? It was eight a.m. and Jessica still hadn't received word from Nathan, and neither had Helena or Amber. Was Mattie's plane late or was she still roasting Nathan for involving his goddaughter in such a risky mission? The Westwood girls had left for the airport to check what was going on as they couldn't get through to Nathan on his mobile.

Buzz! A text message arrived.

Pls come 2 hospital. We need 2 talk about Nathan. Kat xxx.

She tried calling back, but Kat must have immediately turned her phone off. Typical. It was an order, not an invitation. She hesitated. What did Kat want? Was Nathan already there? The girls had instructed her to stay in her cabin but a quick trip to find out exactly what was going on couldn't hurt as long as she kept the cloak with her.

Texting her plans to the Westwood girls, she left the yacht, clutching her holdall tightly. Three armed guards followed.

Father and daughter were locked in an intense conversation in Russian as another set of armed guards allowed Jessica into the private hospital room. Mr Ingorokva was hooked up to drips and monitors; Kat hung tearfully on to his arm. Her sapphire-blue evening dress was crumpled and her hair unbrushed; she couldn't have left his side since he was shot.

"Jessica!" he said weakly. "You wonderful girl. You

saved my life. I don't know how to thank you enough. I am indebted to you and Mr Hall for what you did for me last night."

"He's been here? Nathan, I mean?" She glanced at Kat who brushed a tear from her cheek.

"Earlier this morning. He was on his way to the airport. He said he will debrief me fully later today."

"OK." So Nathan did go to the airport. He was probably still there. So why did Kat want to talk to her about him?

"You must let me give you a token of my gratitude," Mr Ingorokva breathed heavily. "Cash? Diamonds? Or a car? I could buy you a Porsche with personalized number plates if you wish."

"I'm only fourteen and I'm not allowed to drive yet," Jessica said. "Anyway, there's no need to give me anything. I was only doing my job." She stared pointedly at Mr Ingorokva. It was tempting to ask for money to help her dad pay off his mortgage, but she didn't want to be indebted to someone like him. She didn't know what he might ask in return some day.

"Your job?" Kat said. "What do you mean?" She sat bolt upright, frowning hard. "What is she talking about, Papa?"

His face flushed under his daughter's scrutiny.

"I think it's time we all came clean, don't you?" Jessica said. "Particularly you, Mr Ingorokva."

He let out a loud sigh. "Remember, my *kotik*, my little cat – whatever I have done, it's all been for you. I love you so much. You're all I have in the world – well, all that matters anyway."

Kat kissed his hand. "I love you too, Papa."

"You may tell her," he said, nodding at Jessica.

"Your dad employed me to be your undercover bodyguard. He was worried about the death threats and thought you'd be less likely to shake me off than one of your usual bodyguards."

Kat's jaw dropped. "So you were paid to be my friend?"

It was Jessica's turn to redden. "If you want to put it like that, then yes."

"Oh," Kat said. "That explains a few things."

"You mean why I came here when we weren't exactly best mates in New York?"

"I was horrible to you. It didn't make any sense. I thought you were using me. Instead you were spying on me."

"I was helping to keep you safe. And I'd like to think we get on better now. Better than in New York, anyway."

Kat nodded but didn't look totally convinced.

"Thanks to Jessica, the death threats weren't successful," Mr Ingorokva added. "She thwarted Darya and Dr Fedorovna's impersonator."

Kat bit her lip. "You still think they were responsible?"

"It's the most logical explanation," Jessica said. "They both had motive and opportunity."

"Which I helped give them." Kat let out a sob. "I'm so sorry. I should never have given Andrei the combination to my safe or yours, Papa."

Jessica's eyes widened. "You did what?"

"Katyenka has explained everything to me," Mr Ingorokva said, waving his hand dismissively. "She was foolish to trust Dr Fedorovna's imposter, but as I told Mr Hall, that is the extent of her crimes. She is an innocent. She had no idea that he had removed the invisibility cloak from my safe on board *Lilya*.

I suspected something was up when your cabin was targeted by a 'ghost', but the cloak was still there when I double-checked later."

"How did the fake doctor get into the safes in your other properties?" Jessica asked. "The thefts took place all over the world; in New York and Los Angeles."

Mr Ingorokva winced as he exhaled.

"Kat told the doctor about my security codes a while back. All my safes shared the same combination; once he could get into one, he could access them all. It's a security error that has now been remedied. My guards have already checked the timelines against the thefts, and they all coincided with visits from me, Katyenka and our full staff. Dr Fedorovna's impersonator was present on each occasion."

"I still find it hard to believe," Kat spluttered. "He was so genuine."

"All the best con artists appear that way," Jessica said. "That's why they're so good at what they do. Did Nathan say what will happen to you both now?"

"The British Government is willing to waive charges in return for my full cooperation," Mr Ingorokva said, closing his eyes. "It will mean starting a new life in the UK, probably London."

Kat sniffed. "That's what I wanted to ask you, Jessica. Can Mr Hall be trusted? Will he keep his word to us?"

"Of course," she replied. "You can totally trust him. You should take whatever deal he's offering, even if it means moving to London."

Kat's expression was hard to fathom. Was it relief or fear? Maybe relocating to the UK wasn't high up on her wish list but she wouldn't have a choice. Once Mr Ingorokva's Georgian contacts realized he'd double-crossed them by attempting to sell the cloak to their enemies in the opposition party, his life would be in danger. So would Kat's. Again.

They were both lucky to escape charges, but Nathan had been right; MI6 didn't want to advertise that an invisibility cloak, which could bring down governments, even countries, had almost entered the black market.

"I'm curious," Jessica said. "How did you get the cloak?"

Mr Ingorokva's eyes flew open and he fiddled

with the morphine drip. "Scientists in Russia have been working on this technology for a long time. I helped fund the project from its outset, using my late father's money, because I could see its potential. Everyone thought I was mad, including the military. They dismissed the work as far-fetched nonsense, but they were wrong.

"After the fall of the USSR, I took the technology and the scientists with me. They had a breakthrough twelve months ago and created a successful prototype. Within another year or two, I could have had a production line."

"But you decided to sell it instead?"

"I was willing to part with the prototype but not the formula for creating it," he replied. "I'd promised to help the president of Georgia destroy the opposition party. But I came to realize that I'd made a mistake; that many of my business ventures would be placed in jeopardy if that happened."

"Because he'd promised a clampdown on corruption," Jessica said, remembering the newspaper cutting Nathan had sent her.

He held his hands up feebly. "I couldn't afford for

the president to win a second term. I had to protect my interests."

"So you switched sides without telling MI6 because you still wanted protection for Kat? But you weren't selling to the opposition party last night."

"I had no idea that Darya was involved. How could I?"

Jessica didn't doubt him. She'd never have guessed herself.

"I'd arranged to meet a female go-between for the opposition party. I'd never seen the contact before. I wasn't to know that Darya had taken her place." Mr Ingorokva spat the words out and gripped his chest with the effort. "I was duped. Now I have no idea where the cloak is. One thing I'm certain of is that in future, invisibility cloaks will be a staple of modern warfare, thanks to me. Armies will use the technology to coat tanks, making them invisible to the human eye and to radar and radio waves. They will be indispensable to governments. To the British Government, of course. I am now at its disposal."

Jessica's eyes narrowed. Until someone made him another offer he couldn't refuse. It wasn't a good idea to admit that his cloak was in her bag. She didn't trust Mr Ingorokva an inch, even when he was weak and obviously in pain. Neither should Nathan, but maybe he didn't have a choice if he wanted to catch all the players – Margaret, Darya, Allegra and Fake Fed.

"How did the cloak work?" she said curiously. "Do you feel well enough to tell me?"

Mr Ingorokva nodded. "The cloak is a metamaterial, made using nanotechnology, which can change the direction of electromagnetic radiation. Light waves flow around anything hidden beneath the material, as water in a stream flows around a rock, instead of bouncing off the object in the conventional way.

"It means that whatever direction it's viewed from, the light bends around the object or the person behind the cloak, making it look as though they've disappeared. That's the beauty of developments in nanotechnology. Absolutely anything is possible. Imagine it and one day it will come true."

"It's amazing," Jessica breathed.

She'd come across nanotechnology before; the manipulation of particles a millionth the size of a pinhead. Allegra Knight had used the technology in her face cream to speed up the ageing process.

"That's what Nathan said." Mr Ingorokva sank back into his pillows and closed his eyes again. "It's what everyone says."

"Papa's tired and in a lot of pain. He needs his rest. Let me walk you out."

Jessica picked up her bag and followed Kat to the door.

"Papa told me what you did last night," she whispered. "He's convinced that Darya would have killed him if you hadn't been there to stop her."

"Darya's ruthless," Jessica agreed. "I just hope she's caught soon."

Kat shuddered. "Me too." She put her hand on Jessica's arm as she walked into the corridor. "Thank you. You know, for everything."

Wow. That was a first. She'd never heard Kat say thank you for anything. "See you around."

Jessica left the hospital, accompanied by the guards. She checked her mobile in the back seat of the limo. There were some missed calls from Becky but still nothing from Nathan or Mattie. They were the only people she wanted to speak to right now. What should she do? She didn't want to keep the cloak with her for much longer.

Her phone beeped with another text.

Pls call me. I want to sort this mess out. Becky xxx

There was no time for personal stuff. She dropped the phone back into her bag.

Her mobile rang again as the limo pulled up, close to Mr Ingorokva's yacht.

Why couldn't Becky leave her alone? Pulling the mobile out, her eyes lit up as she recognized the number. She climbed out and slammed the door shut.

"Nathan! Where on earth have you been? I've—"

"Come alone to the *Dallas* with the cloak," a familiar voice said. "It's five hundred yards to your left. Tell no one or Nathan and your grandmother will both die. We're monitoring your calls and emails. Ditch your bodyguards. Now."

Allegra Knight hung up. Jessica spun around, clutching her holdall. She scanned the boats and the passers-by. Where was she? Holidaymakers dawdled past and children ate ice cream. Allegra was safely hidden, watching her every move.

Jessica brushed past a guard. "I'm going to buy an ice cream. You don't need to come with me. I'll be quick, I promise."

"We have orders to stay with you," the guard pointed out. "That you have something valuable that needs guarding."

"It's in a bag on my bed. In fact, I need you to check that it's still there. I should never have left it my cabin while I went to the hospital. You need to find it right now."

"Wait here," the man barked.

He led the other guards on to the yacht, leaving her alone. She sprinted along the harbour until she reached a gleaming white speedboat. The *Dallas* was dwarfed by the super yachts docked nearby. She scoured the boat for signs of life but Mattie and Nathan had to be below deck. Were they still alive? Would she be for much longer?

Walking along the gangplank, she knew her dad, Nathan and Mattie would all beg her to turn back. But she couldn't walk away now. She had to do this. If she didn't, Nathan and Mattie would almost certainly end up dead. She had to find a way to save them.

CHAPTER
TWENTY TWO

Jessica gripped the rope and jumped on board. Her stomach lurched and her heart beat wildly.

"Nathan? Are you there? Mattie?"

A slight scuffling noise from below deck made her pause. An ambush was waiting for her, but she had to keep going. What choice did she have? Opening the hatch slowly, she climbed down the stairs. Allegra Knight and whoever else was down there definitely had the advantage. She couldn't see anything until she reached the final few steps.

"No!"

A hand reached out; her foot was wrenched out from beneath her and the bag snatched from her hand. Her head gave a sickening *thud* on the last step before she was dragged along the floor. A tinny noise rang in her ears and something warm and metallic tasting trickled from her nose on to her lips. Blood.

She blinked as she was thrown against something hard. Eventually Mattie came into focus. A tape covered her mouth, and she struggled furiously against the binds that tied her hands and feet together. Next to her was Nathan, also bound and gagged.

"Tie her up – and make sure you do it properly this time," a woman's voice instructed.

Fake Fed lunged into view. Jessica was too weak to fight back. He pinned her arms behind her back and bound her legs, then stepped away to look at his handiwork, revealing Darya stood behind him. Her wounded shoulder was taped up; her right arm in a sling.

"Excellent," she said, waving her gun at Jessica. "Now we can get on with our little fishing expedition. I hope you don't get seasick because this could be a choppy trip."

Jessica closed her eyes. She knew she had concussion. The woman in front of her was Darya yet she sounded exactly like Allegra Knight. She had to be hallucinating. It was hard to focus when the room spun uncontrollably around her.

"Concentrate." A hand slapped her face.

Her eyes flew open again. Darya knelt beside her, smirking. "You're a clever girl. Have you figured it out yet?"

None of this made sense. She heard Allegra but saw Darya; a madwoman who was going to kill them all. Her eyes flitted to the fake doctor. How could she appeal to an assassin to stop this? She had to try. Stalling was the only hope they had while she attempted to get out of her binds. Straining her wrists, she tried to turn on her watch's laser.

"Killing me wasn't part of your orders," she said quietly. "I know it wasn't. Darya isn't in control here. You are."

Darya slapped her again, harder this time. Her fingers slipped from the watch fob. She glanced across the cabin to Nathan and Mattie. Their eyes pleaded with her not to do anything stupid.

"Orders change," Fake Fed said tersely. "Today I follow them." He opened Jessica's Louis Vuitton bag and pulled out the cloak. "She brought it."

"Of course she did," Darya said, chuckling. "Because family means everything to you, doesn't it, Jessica? How is Jack these days? Still trying to work out who killed your beloved mother?"

Jessica gaped at her. How did Darya know about her mum and dad? And why did she sound exactly like Allegra? Her mind whirred as she stared at Fake Fed. She had to concentrate on the facts. The real Dr Fedorovna had been murdered in Brazil six months ago, about the same time that Allegra Knight was spotted in the country, according to MI6 intelligence obtained from Mr Ingorokva.

"Dr Fedorovna ran a plastic surgery clinic and had connections with drug cartels," she murmured.

"You're getting close. But you need to speak up. Nathan and Mattie can't hear you."

The pair stared at Darya, transfixed.

"If you're going to kill her, just do it!" Fake Fed snapped. "She knows too much already."

"I couldn't deny her the chance to figure this out. I want her to die *knowing* that I won."

"Allegra Knight," Jessica said. "It *is* you."

"Correct. But how?"

Jessica stared at her long white fingers and perfectly manicured nails.

"After you went on the run, you ended up in South America," she said slowly. "You paid the real Dr Fedorovna to change your face with plastic surgery."

Surprise flickered over Mattie's face.

"Go on."

"He'd probably done that sort of thing before; I've read about members of drug cartels using plastic surgery to avoid being captured by the police. That's how you've slipped through MI6's facial recognition databases. You didn't look like a glamorous former supermodel; you were Darya, the dowdy, down-beaten tutor to a Russian oligarch. But you forgot one little thing – your hands. Dr Fedorovna didn't alter them, and you continued to look after your nails. They're too well kept for someone who supposedly doesn't care about their appearance."

"True, but it was a small vanity I admit I couldn't bear to lose," Allegra said with a laugh. "But no one noticed apart from you. Mr Ingorokva barely looked at me, as long as I did as I was told and spoke in Russian to Kat."

"Which you taught yourself while you were on the run – to trick Mr Ingorokva into giving you a job?"

"No – I learnt Russian during my modelling career. I've landed the cover of Russian *Vogue* many times. And another minor point I must correct you on – I never paid Dr Fedorovna for the surgery. My friend here had already been contracted to kill him by a drug cartel, unhappy about an official investigation into his taxes that could expose their business dealings."

Jessica shot a look at Fake Fed.

"Don't look so surprised," Allegra said, laughing. "Murder is his business. In fact he was most upset when I surprised him after he'd carried out the hit on Dr Fedorovna. We'd both paid the doctor a late-night visit at his apartment, with the same purpose in mind. He saved me the trouble of killing the doctor myself." Allegra jerked her head at Fake Fed. "He was on the point of killing me too when I struck a deal – my life in return for a generous cut from the recovery and sale of a weapon worth 800 million euros on the black market. Even a hitman couldn't turn down a job as lucrative as that."

"Short of cash were you, Allegra? I never expected you to resurface again."

"I didn't receive my Paris payday from Vectra, thanks to you," she hissed. "I had to be creative. Being on the run and creating a new identity doesn't come cheap."

"I'd say I'm sorry. Except I'm not."

Allegra raised her hand to strike her again.

"So what should I call you now, doctor?" Jessica said quickly, glancing across the cabin. "'Fake Fed' has a certain ring to it, or does it remind you too much of the man you murdered in cold blood?"

"'Dr Fedorovna' suits me fine," he replied. "I might just stick with it a while longer."

Jessica strained against her binds. She had to keep them talking while she tried to escape. "This was the master plan – both of you getting jobs with Mr Ingorokva? You knew he was selling the cloak and were told to cover all fronts; to steal it from him, or if that didn't work out, to turn up at the meeting and swipe it then. Let me guess – was that Margaret's idea?"

"Margaret's always been very resourceful," Allegra

said. "I sent her a coded message while I was on the run. She told me about Mr Ingorokva's cloak and asked me to help her retrieve it so we could sell it to Vectra. We both needed the money, and we always did make a good team."

"Not *that* good," Jessica pointed out. "It must have been a total bummer for you destroying your looks with surgery and then totally failing to get what you wanted. *And* you were shot. Pity Mr Ingorokva wasn't a better aim."

"I got what I wanted in the end," she snarled. "This face was created in months. I can create another one, but you won't live to see it. Your father will never find your body, lost at sea. It will haunt him to his dying day."

Jessica attempted to launch herself at Allegra, but her knees crumbled beneath her.

"We need to get moving," Fake Fed said. "We'll be late for the drop-off with Margaret."

"You're still giving her the cloak?" Jessica asked. "Are you mad? The pair of you will have outlived your usefulness once she gets what she wants – she'll betray you and pocket all the cash from Vectra."

The hitman shot a worried look at Allegra.

"Don't listen to her," she ordered. "Margaret wouldn't dare double-cross us. I told you, she agreed that it's 800 million euros split three ways. She'll be good for it. I promise."

"Dream on," Jessica said. "It's never going to happen."

"Shut up!" Allegra clubbed her over the head with the gun.

Jessica's eyes flickered opened. Her forehead pounded. Taking in her surroundings, she realized the boat's engine was running. Waves bobbed up and down through the porthole opposite. She swivelled around. Mattie and Nathan stared at her, struggling against their restraints. She sat up too quickly. The room spun and bile rose in her throat. She had to bite her lip to stop herself from blacking out again.

"Mattie, I'm so sorry." Jessica coughed up blood. "You should never have got mixed up in this."

Her grandma strained against her gag, trying to answer. Jessica knelt down and shuffled slowly towards her. She reached over and bit the tape binding

Mattie's mouth. Jerking her head back, she pulled the gag off and did the same to Nathan.

"You should never have come," Mattie cried. "Didn't your father teach you anything? Alarm bells should have rung when I didn't text to say I'd arrived and when you couldn't get hold of Nathan."

"It's great to see you too."

"Sorry." Mattie sniffed. "I was praying you'd figure it out and wouldn't come."

"I'm not stupid. I knew they'd kill you if I didn't turn up. I couldn't let that happen. Can you pull the fob on the side of my watch?"

She swivelled around until her wrists touched Mattie's. "Can you feel it?"

"I'm not sure what I'm feeling for," her grandma admitted. Her fingers roamed the watch face. "Is this it?"

Her hands sprung away as a laser activated. Peering over her shoulder, Jessica cut through the binds. Mattie ripped the rope off her ankles and untied Jessica and Nathan. She hugged Jessica briefly.

"That was a little too easy, considering the trouble they took to bring us here," Mattie said, rubbing her wrists.

"Perhaps." Nathan peered out the porthole. "But we're at sea and can't radio for help unless we can get back up on deck." He climbed the stairs and quietly tried the hatch door. "It's locked, and our captors are armed." He paused and came back down the steps, as the sound of a speedboat grew louder.

They peered through the porthole as the boat swung into view. Its engine cut out as it got close enough for someone to jump on board. Jessica held her breath. Maybe Mrs T had figured out what had happened and sent help.

"Is it MI6?" Mattie said tersely.

"In a manner of speaking," Nathan replied. "It's Margaret. She's come to collect the cloak."

Jessica watched as Margaret climbed aboard, clad in a navy trouser suit. Her red Liberty scarf fluttered in the wind. As her jacket flapped open, Jessica spotted a gun tucked into her waistband.

"What's she doing?" Mattie asked. "Will she free us now she has the cloak?"

"Unlikely," Nathan said. "She masterminded the whole thing. She could easily have discovered your travel details and had her hired thugs pick us up from the airport. She also knew Jessica had the cloak. She's got us all where she wants us."

Mattie caught her breath. "So we're loose ends that she—"

Nathan signalled for her to be quiet. He climbed the stairs again and put his ear to the hatch door. Jessica could make out voices directly overhead. It sounded like Margaret, barking orders. The engine died, and a few seconds later a loud *bang* rocked the boat. Jessica and Mattie watched as Margaret hopped back into the speedboat, followed by Fake Fed and Allegra, clutching the Louis Vuitton bag.

"They're leaving," Jessica said.

"That means only one thing. They're going to sink us." Nathan pushed his shoulder against the door. He rammed it again and again. "Quick! Pass me that fire extinguisher!"

Jessica hauled it over. He grabbed it off her and attempted to hammer his way through.

"There's something resting against the door," Nathan said, breathing heavily. "I can't shift it. We need to find another way out."

The speedboat engine started up.

"Stop!" Jessica shouted, hammering on the glass. "You can't leave us here like this!"

Margaret turned and stared at her. She put a hand inside her jacket, pulled out a gun and took aim.

CHAPTER

TWENTY THREE

Jessica ducked as a shot rang out, followed by two more in quick succession. Then there was silence. She peeped out. Margaret was aiming at the boat, not her. Allegra and Fake Fed stood behind her, watching and laughing. Margaret fired off another round.

"She can't have many bullets left," Jessica said.

"Enough to blow us up if she causes a fire in the engine," Nathan replied. "Or sink us. Whichever way, Margaret's making sure the boat's unseaworthy. Even if we manage to get out of this cabin, we can't sail away."

Jessica watched as Margaret spun around, her gun arm rigid. Fake Fed and Allegra were still smiling as the bullets tore through their foreheads. They toppled over the side, splashing face down in the water. The bodies floated, side by side, arms outstretched. Allegra was still clutching her mobile, but Fake Fed's hands were empty. The assassin hadn't seen his own execution coming – he didn't even have time to draw his weapon.

Jessica fell back from the window as the speedboat roared away. "Ohmigod! Allegra and Fake Fed!"

Mattie shook her head. "That was cold-blooded murder."

"Margaret has nothing to lose." Nathan winced as he violently rammed the hatch. "She can't risk leaving anyone alive who can talk."

"Including us." Nausea rose in Jessica's throat.

As Mattie squeezed her hand, there was a sickening judder and the boat lurched violently. Nathan fell down the steps as water gushed into the cabin. Mattie helped Nathan up as Jessica looked around frantically. There must be another way out. Water was rising fast; it had already reached her ankles.

Her eyes rested on the porthole. It was narrow, but she might be able to wriggle out and shift whatever was blocking the hatch.

"It's our only option," Nathan said, following her

gaze. "You're the only one who could fit through. Can you laser it out?"

"I'll try." Jessica flicked on her watch.

A sharp splintering sound ripped through the boat. It lurched again, keeling on to its side. Mattie and Nathan were thrown across the cabin as jets of water spurted around them. Mattie struck a cabinet, hard, and landed face down in the freezing water.

"Mattie!" Jessica waded over and yanked her up. Her eyes were closed, her face deathly pale. Blood gushed from a deep wound above her hairline. The flesh had peeled back to reveal bone. Nathan stood up, blood oozing from a gash on his cheek, and grabbed hold of her grandma, catching his breath as he saw the wound. He leaned over to perform mouth-to-mouth resuscitation. Within a few seconds, water spluttered out of her mouth and her eyes fluttered open.

"I th-th-thought we'd lost you," Jessica said, her teeth chattering.

Mattie tried to speak but coughed up blood.

"Laser the window," Nathan panted. "I'll hold Mattie."

They were sinking fast; the water had lapped over

the porthole outside and almost reached Jessica's shoulders. Within seconds, they'd be completely submerged. But even if she could laser through the porthole and get out, Nathan and Mattie could never squeeze through. Chances were she wouldn't be able to shift whatever was blocking the hatch door either if it was already below water. What kind of rubbish plan was this when she couldn't get Nathan and Mattie out?

"Why are we—?" She stopped as she saw the look on Nathan's face. "No. I'm not doing it."

"You have to go," he insisted. "You've still got a chance. We don't. Your father would want this."

"We all go together or not at all. I'm not leaving you."

"Stop being so bloody pig-headed." Nathan spat out a mouthful of water. "Get out of that porthole. That's an order. We've run out of options."

"No. We haven't." She raised her arm out the water.

"Dear God." His eyes locked on her explosive bracelet. "I never dreamt you'd actually have to use that thing."

Neither had Jessica, but if she managed to blast a

hole in the boat, they could pull Mattie out and swim to the surface. It was a big "if"; the explosion could kill them, or injure them so badly that they wouldn't be able to swim.

What did they have to lose? Within minutes, they'd drown anyway.

"Let's do this carefully," he said. "I'll talk you through it step by step."

Jessica trod water, holding her head as high as possible, as she undid the bracelet. Fumbling with numb fingers, it slipped from her grasp.

"No!" She dived beneath the surface. The water was murky and full of floating objects. Groping around her, she grabbed a lamp and then a bag.

Got it! Her fingers curled around the chain and she kicked back to the surface. There was hardly any air left in the cabin; she had to float on her back and tip her head to breathe.

This time, she was more careful. She couldn't afford another mistake. She held the bracelet out the water.

"Pull the heart charm and rotate it three times anti-clockwise to activate the explosives," Nathan said.

Jessica obeyed. Next, she followed his instructions

and snapped open a cat charm. A long, syringe-like needle shot out.

"Stab it into the wall. It looks fragile but it's made from a compound stronger than steel. Shove it in as hard as you can."

Jessica took a deep breath and dived down, attaching the bracelet below the porthole. She emerged again, gasping. "How long do we have?"

"Thirty seconds," he replied, spitting out water. "We need to get as far away as possible from the blast."

Together, they supported Mattie's head and swam across the cabin as the water lapped over their heads.

Ten, nine, eight, seven, six, Jessica counted as she held her breath. *Five, four, three, two, one.*

Nothing. Maybe the bracelet had fallen off and deactivated. She wanted to scream but couldn't open her mouth. Nathan's fingers curled over hers and squeezed her hand. Back in the airport, he'd explained that the bracelet was an early prototype. Now wasn't a good time to discover it didn't work. She shook off his hand.

Letting go of Mattie, Jessica kicked towards the

bracelet. Nathan grabbed her wrist again, attempting to pull her back, but she wrestled free. The bracelet had to be activated. She swam into a blinding flash of white and an ear-splitting *boom*. Pieces of splintered wood exploded around her as she was flung backwards like a rag doll.

White foam filled her eyes and she was sloshed around as if she were in a giant washing machine, sharp objects tearing at her body. She had no idea which direction to start swimming in.

Mattie! she screamed inwardly. *Nathan!*

She stretched her arms out and searched blindly for them, but they had been swept away. Her lungs were at bursting point. She had to get out.

Something grabbed her wrist.

No! She twisted and kicked, but the hand clung on. Had Margaret returned to finish her off? Desperately trying to pull away, she caught a glimpse of long red hair and goggles. The woman's eyes behind the mask were wide-eyed, begging her to stop fighting. She pulled off her oxygen mask and put it over Jessica's mouth and nose. Signalling upwards, she held on to her and shared the oxygen as they kicked.

Jessica broke through the surface and took a desperate gulp of air. She immediately recognized the diver as Helena, one of the Westwood models.

"Hold on," the girl ordered. "We'll get you out of here."

Helena pulled her towards a white boat. A pair of hands reached down and dragged her aboard. Jessica flopped on to her back on the deck, panting.

"You have to get Nathan and Mattie," she gasped. "They're still down there."

"It's OK, they've just been brought aboard." Helena jerked her head over her shoulder. Mattie and Nathan lay on the deck, coughing, as they were given first aid.

Jessica tried to sit up. "Are they going to be all right?"

Helena gently eased her down again. "You need to rest. Their injuries aren't life-threatening, but they need to get to hospital. You too."

Tears welled in Jessica's eyes. They were all safe. The risk had paid off. She wiped her eyes and shielded them from the sun's glare. "How did you find us?"

The smell of antiseptic filled her nostrils as Helena leant over and dabbed a wound on her face with a cloth. She hadn't realized she was injured until now. Every part of her body hurt.

"We placed a tracking device on your Louis Vuitton bag back at the yacht. We knew something was wrong when we couldn't reach Nathan and discovered you were heading out to sea with the holdall."

"Where is it now?" Propping herself up on her elbows, she noticed that her jeans were ripped to shreds and she'd lost both sandals.

"We retrieved it from Margaret," Helena replied. "But not before a gun battle."

She nodded over her shoulder. Margaret lay on the deck, streaked with blood, as a woman tended to her. Amber stood close by, clutching the Louis Vuitton bag as she talked to two armed men.

"Is Margaret…?" Jessica's voice trailed off.

"No, she's not dead. We wanted to take her alive. She took a bullet to her thigh. That's all."

Jessica struggled to her feet. "So it's over? Definitely?"

"It is for Margaret," a familiar voice said.

Jessica spun round and was enveloped into Nathan's bloodied arms. A hug was definitely what she needed right now; she just hadn't expected it from her godfather.

"Margaret won't get away with it this time, I promise you," he said. "She faces a life sentence without the chance of parole."

Jessica glanced across at Margaret. Her eyes flickered open briefly. A smile curled on her lips.

CHAPTER
TWENTY FOUR

The towering clothes mountain in the corner of Kat's cabin was horribly familiar; they followed her wherever she went around the world.

"I have absolutely nothing to wear," Kat wailed. "I need a whole new wardrobe for Tokyo and London. I can't take any of *this* with me." She pulled a disgusted face.

Jessica suppressed a giggle as the pile collapsed. Some things never changed. "Not even the Armani?" She pointed to a short scarlet cocktail dress and stole from this season's catwalk shows. Fashionistas around the world would kill for this outfit, not to mention the girls back at school.

Kat followed her gaze. "OK, well maybe I'll take

that." She snatched up the dress and threw it on to the bed in a crumpled ball. "But the rest…" She waved her hand dismissively. "I don't know where to begin. Maybe I'll get the maid to sort it out for me. She can help you too if you like."

"Thanks, but I'm done already." It hadn't taken long to pack for London; Jessica didn't possess every item in this season's designer collections. She was more than ready for her flight. Mr Ingorokva had arranged for a private plane to take her, Nathan and Mattie home while he and Kat went to the Tokyo photo shoot in his jet.

"Are you sure?" Kat raised a perfectly plucked eyebrow. "I peeked next door. You haven't packed the clothes Papa bought you yet." She grabbed a lipstick off her dresser and reapplied a slick of red gloss in the mirror. "They were hand-picked by Clara and cost hundreds of thousands of euros, you know."

How could she forget? Mr Ingorokva had deliberately left the receipt for her to find during her first night on the yacht. When would she ever wear those ostrich feathers and padded-shoulder gowns? An eighties fancy dress party, maybe. Better to find a diplomatic way of saying her stylist's taste in clothes totally sucked.

"I think I'll leave the clothes here, if you don't mind. It's not the kind of stuff I wear back home. It's not like I ever go to anything formal."

Kat looked aghast. "Not even cocktail parties?"

"I'm more of a gigs kind of girl."

A Jamie's gigs kind of girl, she wanted to add. Or she used to be, before the whole Jamie-getting-off-with-Becky thing blew up in her face.

"Leave the clothes then," Kat said. "It means you can travel light, next time you come and visit me here."

"Er, hang on a minute. Did I hear right? I'm being invited back?"

Kat giggled. "Of course. We're friends now, aren't we? Even after everything that's happened, you know, like you going behind my back and spying on me."

"And me having to dig *you* out of particularly large holes," Jessica pointed out. "Such as helping you avoid a criminal record."

Kat blushed. "Truce?"

"Truce."

Kat giggled as she picked up a silk aquamarine jumpsuit. "Keep or bin?"

"Keep. Why throw away something you've had less than a week?"

Kat smirked as she threw it at her. "I'm binning it but you can have it if you want. Papa will buy me a whole new wardrobe when we finally relocate to London. He's already booked a personal shopper at Harvey Nicks. I can't wait to get started. I'm thinking of cutting off all my hair and trying a new look." She scraped her hair away from her face. "What do you think?"

"You're the kind of person who'd look good completely bald and wearing a sack." Jessica flung herself down on the bed and opened her handbag.

"Ha! You're right, of course," Kat chortled. "I can't help it. I take after mama. Papa said she turned heads wherever she went."

Jessica checked her mobile as Kat rummaged through a large Louis Vuitton trunk. She didn't have any new texts, but Becky had updated Facebook with photos of her rehearsals for the National Youth Theatre's production of *Romeo and Juliet*. Wow.

Becky must have landed that role after she'd flown to Monaco. Good for her. She couldn't help but feel proud as she scrolled through the pictures. It explained why Becky had been so hard to get hold of in New York; she'd been tied up in rehearsals.

"Oh, no!"

"What is it?" Kat threw a skirt and three blouses on to her "bin" pile, price tags still attached.

"I've screwed up," Jessica said slowly. "Big time."

She stared at the picture of Becky kissing Jamie and sticking two fingers up behind his head.

Thanks to Jamie, my Romeo stand-in, Becky had posted. *Leading man back in a few days. Get well soon, Rob. The balcony's not the same without you! xx*

They were wearing the same shirts in the photo that had been texted to her. Becky hadn't been messing about with Jamie; he'd stepped in to help her rehearse her lines when the actor was off sick. The photo was from Romeo and Juliet's first kiss on the balcony. Jessica's stomach churned horribly. How could she have accused her best friend of betraying her like that? Becky had tried to explain but she'd refused to listen.

"I'm such a doofus," she groaned.

"I could have told you that, but what have you done exactly?"

Jessica gave a brief account, starting with the photo a troublemaker had texted.

"Uh-oh," Kat said. "Sounds like you need to start grovelling. Big time."

"I know. I should call Becky now and beg her to give me a second chance. Jamie too."

"I'm sure you'll be able to persuade them." Kat gestured around the room. "Why don't you pick something out for your friend? Take what you want. Most of this stuff is brand new."

Jessica eyed the clothes. Becky would seriously love some of this gear, but she knew she couldn't buy her friend off the way Kat usually did to people. She owed Becky a massive apology, not a new bag.

Kat hauled out yet more Louis Vuitton luggage from the wardrobe and emptied them.

"What would your friend like?" she persisted. "A dress? A blouse? A new handbag? I have plenty. None of this stuff has been worn yet. It's all tagged so she'll think you bought it."

"Thanks, but I need to call her."

"Sure thing. Then give her a teeny weeny present. You might as well. I'm only going to throw all this stuff out if you don't want it."

Jessica's eyes widened. It was totally gross the way Kat frittered away money. Surely she could sell what she didn't want or give it away to charity? Or maybe Jessica could do that. She could auction off the clothes and donate the money to something worthwhile. Like eat-humble-pie.com or a charity of Becky or Jamie's choice.

She pulled out a large cream Victoria Beckham handbag from the pile of clothes as Kat wandered into the bathroom. The bag was totally gorgeous and way more expensive than anything she or any of her friends could ever afford. Jessica turned it over. She recognized the hole in the bottom. This was the bag Kat had tripped over in the hotel; it had been splashed with sulphuric acid but wasn't too badly damaged. Someone would probably still buy it for the label.

She checked to make sure that Kat hadn't left anything inside, like a pair of diamond earrings. Her hand caught on the lining. That was odd. The material was badly ripped and eaten away by acid, yet the hole in the leather was comparatively small. It didn't make any sense. How could the acid have destroyed the fabric on the inside of Kat's bag? She felt something lumpy in the next compartment. Unzipping it, she saw a silver hip flask that was engraved: TO MY DARLING LEVAN, ALL MY LOVE, LILYA XXXX.

It was a present from Kat's late mum to Mr Ingorokva. She didn't want to open the bottle; judging from damage to the surrounding material, it could contain acid. How? Fake Fed couldn't have kept the acid in Kat's bag without her knowing. It didn't make sense. Using her compact, she lifted three fingerprints off the bottle while Kat sang loudly and out of tune in the bathroom. She fished her iPad out of her handbag and logged on as Kat emerged carrying fistfuls of lipsticks.

"So will you show me the sights when I get to London?" Kat said, without looking up.

"Sure, if you want." Jessica noticed masses of Facebook posts about Jamie's gig she hadn't read yet. They would have to wait a bit longer. She was behind with other things too; the last few days had been so manic she'd forgotten to run the fingerprints she'd lifted from the safe in Kat's cabin.

"You'd probably like Madame Tussauds and the Tower of London," she said, concentrating hard.

While Kat wasn't watching, she balanced her compact on her iPad. She hoped Nathan hadn't pulled the plug on her access to confidential files yet. The iPad picked up a signal and within seconds, she was inside the MI6 computer system. Brill.

"I was thinking more about some hot clubs and bars you could take me to," Kat said, examining a sheer black dress.

"Of course." Jessica uploaded the data she'd collected from the safe and the bottle in Kat's handbag and ran it against Fake Fed's fingerprints that had been kept on file.

No match.

She caught her breath. Fake Fed hadn't touched the stolen booty or the hip flask. He wasn't the cat burglar or the person who'd tried to kill Kat with sulphuric acid. This time, she did a cross-check against all of Mr Ingorokva's employees; Margaret had demanded fingerprints from everyone on board *Lilya*, including Darya or rather Allegra masquerading as Darya.

Again no match. So she wasn't involved either.

There were only two people left she hadn't tried; Mr Ingorokva himself and Kat. Margaret had kept copies of their fingerprints too.

She hit the search button. A few seconds later, there was a *ping*.

Match found.

Heart beating rapidly, she opened the file.

Katyenka Ingorokva.

"It was you all along," Jessica gasped.

"Do you mean the shoot in Tokyo?" Kat said breezily. "Yes, I thought I was the best at the casting but you never know, do you?" Kat threw the lipsticks on to the bed, next to Jessica. "You can take these too."

"I don't want them." She swiped them off the silk duvet. "You played me. You blamed Dr Fedorovna for the thefts and the attempts on your life but it was you."

"Are you mad?" Kat retorted.

She stalked over to the wardrobe door and slammed

it shut. "You can't make up lies like that. Papa is well-connected. He could get people to—"

"They're not lies," Jessica interrupted. "I've got proof. I lifted fingerprints from the stuff in your safe. Your precious doctor didn't touch anything."

"That's probably because he wore gloves. Didn't you think about that, Sherlock?"

"Yes, but you didn't," she pointed out. "That was your first big mistake. Your fingerprints are on Madison Matthew's necklace, the Frick museum ornament and the other stolen jewellery."

Kat clamped her hands on her hips and tossed her hair over her shoulder. "OK, I lied. So what? I went to put mama's bracelet away one night and found all that stuff in my safe. I didn't grass up Andrei. Big deal. MI6 isn't pressing charges, so what does it matter?"

"Because you're still lying. How do you explain this?"

She lifted up Kat's handbag. "Your bag's burned from the inside because you put sulphuric acid in your dad's hip flask. Silver isn't destroyed by acid, but it leaked. Your fingerprints are all over it. I bet if I searched your cabin, I'd find the paper and newspaper cuttings you used to make the death threats."

Kat's bottom lip trembled. "I have no idea what you're talking about."

"Yes, you do," Jessica insisted. "You faked the attempt on your life. I remember stepping on ice cubes when I picked up your handbag. You emptied the glass of ice while no one was watching and filled it with sulphuric acid. You deliberately tripped to spill the acid but it splashed your hand."

Kat shook her head vigorously. "You're wrong."

"You wrote the death threats to your dad and came into my cabin that night, wearing the invisibility cloak, and using your dad's master key card," Jessica continued. "You'd already used the cloak to carry out the thefts. But why? Did you get some kind of sick thrill out of it? Or were you so desperate for your dad's attention that you had to fake everything?"

Kat burst into tears and slumped on to the bed.

"So that's it. All of this to get a few minutes of your dad's time."

"You've no idea what it's like." Mascara streaked down Kat's cheeks. "Papa barely notices I'm here. He gives me his credit card and I can buy whatever I want, but I can't buy his attention. He won't give me that. Not willingly."

"He loves you."

"Does he? Maybe. But he loves his business and his money more. He didn't even come to visit me in hospital when I burnt my hand. He was too busy."

"He was worried sick."

Jessica remembered the look on Kat's face when she realized how concerned her dad had been. She'd looked excited, elated even.

"You enjoyed seeing your dad so het up," she added.

Kat nodded vigorously. "Can you blame me? He talked to me; he spent a bit more time with me. It was worth it." She fiddled with the bandage on her hand. "No one got hurt, except me, and Papa noticed me for the first time in months. He actually knew I existed."

"So you let Dr Fedorovna take the rap for threatening to kill you and carrying out the robberies?" Jessica frowned. Kat hadn't known that Fake Fed was a ruthless hitman for hire who'd murdered the real Dr Fedorovna.

"It was the obvious thing to do," Kat said, with a

shrug. "I'd known for a while that he wasn't who he said he was. He claimed he owned a plastic surgery clinic, yet he knew next to nothing about collagen fillers. He bluffed quite well when I asked him how long they lasted before needing to be redone, but I knew he was winging it."

"So why didn't you report him to your dad?"

"Andrei was *soo* pretty," she replied. "And I knew he'd be useful to have around if I ever got caught with stolen goods. It'd be easy to believe that a man who'd taken a job under false pretences was actually the cat burglar."

Jessica gaped. Cold or what? Kat had never cared for Fake Fed; she'd been using him all along. They'd both had hidden motives for getting to know each other.

"You wanted your dad's attention but that doesn't explain why you stole all that jewellery and the Frick ornament. You have everything you could ever possibly want and more. So why do it?"

Kat snorted. "You don't get it, do you? That bit was a game, a diversion, whatever you want to call it. It was fun."

"Not for the people you robbed," Jessica said. "Didn't you ever think of them?"

"They weren't so badly affected. They could claim on their insurance, couldn't they?"

Jessica shook her head. "That's hardly the point. You broke into that heiress's hotel room in Monaco; she was probably traumatized by the theft."

"Of course you wouldn't understand, Miss Goody Two-Shoes," Kat snarled. "You're probably the only person in the world who hasn't thought what they'd do for a day if they had an invisibility cloak."

"I wouldn't steal. I know that."

"I was *borrowing*," Kat corrected. "I always intended to return everything one day. But it became harder and harder to get hold of Papa's cloak without being caught as he increased his security. I could hardly march into the Frick museum in broad daylight and put the vase back, could I?"

"How did you find the cloak? Did your dad tell you about it?"

"As if! I was telling the truth. I knew his combination and it worked on all his safes around the world. I often sneaked a look at what he was keeping locked up; important documents, jewels, even a gun. Then one night I found the cloak. I knew he'd never let me borrow something so valuable even if I begged. I took it with me on the morning of the Grammys. Papa had bought me a seat at the show and I was dying to see Madison Matthews up close. I'd read about her amazing necklace and visited her hotel before the ceremony." She closed her eyes. "Madison looked breathtaking. I think she saw me, once or twice. She was really jumpy that day in her suite. She was terrified someone would steal the necklace."

"Which you did. Live on TV."

"I wanted to see if I could get away with it," Kat admitted. "And I did. Time and time again. It's unbelievably cool that everyone thought a ghost was on the loose in New York, and that the ghost was me."

"That's what you were doing when you went ashore the other night? You weren't going to a casino, you robbed that woman. You're the cat burglar."

"I thought you were supposed to be a spy? Didn't you get the clue? Cat burglar, Kat burglar? *Kotik*, my little cat?"

"Clearly not. I trusted you for some reason."

Kat's eyes gleamed. "I don't usually get much excitement. Papa sees to that. I have no friends my age, only employees to talk to. I'm chaperoned everywhere by bodyguards, tutors and nannies. My life is unbelievably dull."

"It's no excuse for what you've done."

"Stop judging me," Kat hit back. "You don't know what it's like. I have everything yet I have nothing. Papa doesn't want to know me and my mother is dead." Her voice trembled. "Murdered."

"Mine too," said Jessica. "At least your family got justice. The people who killed your mum are in jail, but whoever killed mine got away with it."

"I know," Kat said sharply.

Jessica's voice wavered. "What do you mean?"

"I heard Papa talking to one of his security guards. He did a background check before you came aboard. Papa knew all about you and your family of spies. It was most interesting, I have to say."

"What?" Jessica caught her breath. "So you knew all along that I was here to spy on you? Your outrage in the hospital was fake along with everything else?"

"Papa always says keep your friends close and your

317

enemies closer. Spying on the spy was fun. I had a good read when Papa put your family's file back in his safe."

Jessica scowled. She longed to grab Kat by the shoulders and shake her hard. She fought to control her temper. "What do you know?"

A smile hovered on Kat's glossy red lips. "If you want to find out about Vectra's involvement in your mother's death, it's time we struck a deal, Jessica Cole."

Kat wasn't bluffing. She'd never mentioned the name Vectra to her before. "What do you want?" she asked.

"Isn't it obvious? You forget our little conversation and destroy all the evidence that links me to the thefts and the death threats. In return, I'll tell you what I know about your mother and Vectra."

Jessica clenched her fists. Now she wanted to strangle her. Kat had put her in an impossible position. MI6 had returned the stolen items to their owners and the case was closed, with the blame resting on the fake doctor. Kat deserved to be punished, but she would get away with it if Jessica didn't turn her in. Also, if she didn't report her, she'd be an accessory after the fact.

But what if Kat had information that could help her track down her mum's killer?

"Well? I need an answer, Jessica. You have a plane to catch and so do I. The clock is ticking."

"OK," she said stiffly. "It's a deal."

"So hand over my bag and destroy the fingerprints."

Jessica clutched the bag to her stomach. Was she really going to do this?

"Do it, or there's no deal," Kat said, holding out her hand. "Tick tock, tick tock."

Jessica's hand shook slightly as she held it out. Kat snatched the bag from her.

"Now the fingerprints. Bin them."

She called up the file of prints she'd lifted. Was she doing the right thing? Didn't she have to think of the bigger picture? Her finger hovered over the delete button for a few seconds. She closed her eyes and pressed.

"Done," she said, showing Kat the screen. "Now talk."

Kat did a search on her name and brought up "zero results".

"I don't know much," she admitted. "Papa told the

319

guard your mother was investigating Vectra when she died."

"I know that already. I backed up my files on here, you know. I can always restore the fingerprints if you don't keep up your side of the bargain."

"OK. Papa said she'd found out something that Vectra was willing to kill for. Something called 'Sargasso'."

"What's that?"

"I've no idea. Papa didn't say. He mentioned he knew a former KGB agent who'd stumbled on Sargasso. He'd been murdered too, along with others."

"Did he give a name? Who were the others?"

Kat looked away. "That's all I know."

Jessica stared at her. "I think you know more than you're letting on. You read the file in your dad's safe. What did it say?"

Kat met her gaze. "Actually, I made a copy of the file and kept it."

"So give it me."

"Why? I don't take orders from you."

"Please," Jessica said. "I'm begging you. If you won't give it to me, give it to MI6. It could help bring Vectra to justice."

Kat threw her head back and laughed loudly. "I never thought I'd hear the great Jessica Cole begging. But I have to ask myself, what's in this for me? If Vectra is as dangerous as everyone says, why would I want to get involved?"

"Maybe because you have a conscience? And it's the right thing to do?"

"That's where you're wrong," Kat said icily. "I don't have a conscience. I have to look after number one. I'll deny ever having this conversation if you tell anyone at MI6 about Sargasso and I'll destroy the file."

"But—"

"This is my insurance policy." Kat picked up a brush and ran it through her long mane. "In case you ever retrieve that fingerprint file or talk to anyone about me."

"I won't. I promise."

"Still, you never know. I might need a favour in the future. Now I know exactly who to call."

CHAPTER
TWENTY FIVE

"Would you care for any refreshments?"

Jessica opened her eyes and stared up at the air steward, who was clad in a red waistcoat and black bow tie. The dark-haired man smiled, revealing nicotine-stained teeth. "The orange juice is freshly squeezed or I can recommend the mocha lattes."

"Orange juice is fine, thank you," Jessica said, taking a glass off the tray.

She noticed a tiny tattoo of an eye between his thumb and finger as she sipped her juice. OK, so it wasn't Mr Ingorokva's huge luxurious jet, but this was still pretty cool. It was a small private plane with only Nathan and Mattie on board, along with the two Westwood models and two of Mr Ingorokva's armed guards whom he'd loaned for the flight. He'd also spared a minimal crew – the pilot and Mark, the in-flight attendant who'd served her.

There was also Margaret, of course. How could Jessica forget her? She threw a glance over her shoulder. Margaret was handcuffed to a seat at the back of the plane; her eyes were closed and she was doped up with painkillers. She'd refused to speak since being arrested, and Nathan doubted she'd cooperate with MI6 back in London. However, they had more than enough evidence to charge her. He said she'd stand trial for murder, attempted murder and treason, when she was well enough. But first she was being transferred to a hospital for treatment to her injured leg.

Mark placed a basket of warm pastries on the table and took Nathan and Mattie's drink orders.

"What time are we expected to land at London Heathrow?" Jessica said.

"In approximately two hours," he replied. "We have perfect flying conditions today so it should be a pleasant flight."

Mattie closed her eyes and stretched out. She still made an effort with her appearance – a dusty pink

Chanel suit and diamond accessories – despite the large bandage around her head. She'd needed half a dozen stitches but thankfully hadn't suffered concussion.

"I certainly hope so," Mattie murmured. "I've never cared for flying unless it's first class or a private plane of course. Then I can almost bear it."

"I guess we have something to thank Mr Ingorokva for," Nathan said, laughing. "He's not all bad."

He wasn't all good either, and neither was his daughter. Jessica glanced out the window as she sensed Mattie's eyes boring into her face. She'd managed to keep Kat's secret from Nathan, but Mattie was a tough cookie. She'd been resting up since Allegra's attack and they hadn't had much chance to talk in private. However, Mattie had a sixth sense about these sorts of things. Back at the airport, she'd asked Jessica whether she was holding something back. Of course, she'd denied it.

Would her path cross with Kat's in London? Jessica wouldn't hold her breath. They didn't exactly move in the same social circles, and Kat would probably attempt to give her a wide berth until she wanted to call in her favour. If only she could find out more about Sargasso. A quick trawl through MI6 files – before she lost her clearance – hadn't produced any results. However, she was only allowed into a tiny part of the system; there could be something confidential buried in highly restricted folders she couldn't access.

"Can you pass me a pastry, please? I can't stretch." Nathan jangled the chain attaching his wrist to the briefcase containing the invisibility cloak. He'd been handcuffed to the case since they left Monaco under armed guard. Mrs T was happy for Nathan to deliver the cloak, instead of the military.

Jessica handed over a pain aux raisins. "I hope you don't lose the key."

"It's perfectly safe, thank you," he said, patting his jacket pocket.

"OW!" She leapt to her feet as a milky latte splashed down her legs.

"I'm terribly sorry." Mark regained his balance as the plane lurched. He placed the half-empty cup down in front of Mattie.

"Are you OK? Let me get some tissues for you."

"No, it's fine. I'll clean it up in the bathroom." Jessica stood up, brushing herself down. Her jeans were wet through.

"I thought you said it'd be a smooth flight?" Mattie said.

"Apologies again. We're experiencing a little turbulence but it should pass. I'll make you another latte." He turned to Jessica. "I'm so sorry, Miss. Are you sure there's nothing I can do?"

"No, honestly. I've got a spare pair of trousers with me." Jessica reached over and grabbed her vanity case. "Don't eat all the pastries." She winked at Mattie.

The Westwood girls smiled as she brushed past to the bathroom. The bodyguards remained buried behind their newspapers. Jessica raised an eyebrow as she caught the headline:

MYSTERY AS FRICK VASE TURNS UP ON CURATOR'S DOORSTEP OVERNIGHT.

Madison Matthews had probably received a similar night-time visit too.

Jessica locked herself into the bathroom and changed into a pair of black tracksuit bottoms; she'd been meaning to put them on. They were far more comfortable to travel in. She scrubbed at her jeans with soap and a flannel. Hopefully they'd dry out before they landed. She changed into her trainers too as her silver pumps didn't look right with something so casual.

Rummaging in her vanity case for her brush, her fingers ran over her gadgets – the sunglasses, jewellery and hairspray. Would Nathan ask for them back? Maybe she'd be invited to join Westwood again now Margaret was out of the picture.

Whooaa!

The vanity case leapt in the air as the plane plummeted. Towels rained down from the overhead cupboard, along with toiletries. Jessica gasped for breath as the air tightened in her chest. Within seconds, the oxygen was sucked from the cabin.

She clawed through her case, seized her necklace and managed to get it over her head. Putting it to her mouth, she inhaled and filled her lungs with air.

Thank God. The device didn't just work underwater. Clutching the door handle, Jessica tugged at it. It was jammed shut as if it'd been locked from the outside. What was going on out there? She slammed into the wall as the plane lurched again, her ears popping painfully as the pressure fell. They were losing altitude fast. At this rate, they were going to crash.

Sucking on her pendant, Jessica aimed the watch laser at the lock and burned through the door. She kicked it open and staggered out. Trays and food were scattered across the floor. She lurched towards the cockpit. The door flew open as she pushed against it.

The pilot was slumped against the controls, his face blue. An oxygen mask swung from the ceiling. *Ohmigod.* She shook him and placed the mask over his face. His eyes rolled open briefly and closed again. *Wake up!* Shaking him violently again, she glanced about. Emergency lights flashed across the control panel. Where was Mark? Mr Ingorokva said the flight attendant doubled as the co-pilot. But if he hadn't managed to get his mask on in time, he'd be unconscious too. No one else had made it into the cockpit. That probably meant they couldn't. They'd passed out. That left her.

Jessica sucked deeply into her pendant. What should she do? Sure, her dad used to fly and had paid for her to take a few lessons for her last birthday, but boy did that seem a long time ago. There was no way she could land this thing. The dials on the altitude and speed indicators spun out of control as the aircraft dived. Grabbing the control stick, she tried to pull up the plane's nose. The autopilot; that's what she needed. At least that would stabilize the plane. What had her instructor told her? Her mind raced as she scanned the flashing control panel. There was no autopilot button. It wasn't as easy as it looked in movies. She closed her eyes and tried to picture the control panel in the light aircraft she'd taken her lessons in. Her instructor had pointed out the flight director mode switch, for use in emergencies.

Her eyes flew open. There it was! There were three levels – off, on and auto – but which one actually flew the plane? If she remembered rightly, on didn't move the plane wings; it enabled the pilot to follow wings on the artificial horizon ahead, mimicking the guidance from the autopilot. That was no good to her. It had to be auto. She stared at the altitude meter; they were fast approaching ten thousand feet. Jessica's finger hovered over the auto switch. If they could descend to this height, there would be enough oxygen to breathe. But how long would it take the plane to stabilize? She had no idea. She turned the button and watched the gauge as the descent slowed. The speed dropped and the plane lined up with the artificial horizon. The plane was levelling. It was the best she could hope for.

She felt for the pilot's pulse and found a weak tremor under her fingertips. It was doubtful he'd be in a fit state to fly even if she were able to revive him. She had to find someone who could take over.

Oxygen masks swung from the ceiling as she made her way into the cabin. They'd all been activated as soon as they started to lose altitude. Drinks, papers and bags lay scattered about. The Westwood girls slumped over in their seats and the bodyguards lay in the aisle. It looked like they'd attempted to get to the cockpit before they passed out. Jessica pulled them into sitting up positions and managed to get oxygen masks on them all.

Mattie! She climbed over the guards to her table. Mattie lay across the seat, her face blue.

No! Jessica pushed her up, tipping her head back. She sucked on her pendant and blew the oxygen into her mouth. As soon as her eyelids moved, she clamped on the mask. Mattie's eyes slowly opened.

"Hold this tight," Jessica ordered. "The oxygen should return to the cabin soon."

Mattie weakly clutched the mask, inhaling deeply.

"Where's Nathan?" she said, looking around. His briefcase was gone too.

Mattie pointed down the plane. Margaret's seat was empty. Her handcuffs were open, dangling from the armrest. She'd managed to free herself and sabotage the aircraft to get the invisibility cloak. But how did she expect to survive the crash?

Jessica staggered towards the baggage hold. The door was locked. Within seconds, her watch had seared through the metal. She burst through the door and was immediately knocked off her feet. Her pendant flew from her mouth. She clung desperately to the door as her legs flew from beneath her. The hatch door was open, sucking suitcases and bags out. Nathan hung on to a luggage belt, his eyes wide open with terror.

Standing by the hatch was Mark, strapped into a parachute harness and clutching Nathan's briefcase, the handcuff dangling loose. Margaret clung on nearby. Neither wore face masks. Jessica spat out her pendant. They must have reached ten thousand feet. She could breathe without assistance.

"We had a deal, Vectra!" Margaret screamed. "I delivered the cloak as promised, now give me a parachute."

Vectra! Jessica stared at the flight attendant. She'd only ever seen a blurred black-and-white photo of him. He looked far younger in person and more, well, normal. Not the satanic-looking figure she'd built up in her head. The monster that'd murdered her mum.

"Get your own," he spat back. "There's one parachute left for whoever can reach it first." He jerked his head back towards a rucksack, hanging from a rack close to Jessica. "I don't care either way."

"You son-of-a—" Margaret began. "We agreed I'd get the full 800 million euros with Allegra and the doctor out of the picture."

"The terms have changed," Vectra shouted. "You've exposed the operation and become a liability. You get nothing."

Margaret attempted to move towards Jessica but the force dragged her back towards the hatch.

"I'll kill you for this," she screeched

"I doubt that," Vectra returned. "But you're welcome to try. I'm always ready." He held the parachute cord, poised to leap out.

"No! Wait!"

Vectra turned and stared at Jessica, still gripping the briefcase containing the invisibility cloak. A smile crept across his face. "Jessica Cole. It's a pity it has to end like this for you. You'd have been an asset to my network."

"Dream on," she yelled back. "I know you killed my mum."

Vectra smirked. "Goodbye. We won't meet again." He braced himself in the hatch doorway, preparing to leap.

"Sargasso!" she called after him.

"What?" Vectra half-turned, shock registered on his face as he fell, holding the briefcase.

Quick as a flash, Margaret tried to lever her way towards the rucksack, hooking her hands through luggage railings. Nathan let go and slipped head first towards the hatch, attempting to stop her.

"No!" Jessica cried.

Dangling by one hand, she pulled the lever on her watch and aimed it above her head. The nanowire shot out and hooked over the railing with a mini grapnel.

Jessica let go and slid towards the hatch, grabbing hold of Nathan's ankle. He was half out, arms flailing.

"AAAGH!" Her arms were being ripped from their sockets. Her watch had tightened around her wrist. The force from the door was unbearable. She couldn't hold on to Nathan much longer.

He clawed at the door with his free hand. A grapnel shot out of his watch and hooked around the handle. He had the same gadget! Heaving on it, he slowly pulled the door. Jessica fell to the floor as it finally closed.

"You did it, Nathan!"

She looked up. Margaret was already scrambling for the rucksack, holding her injured leg. Jessica grabbed her foot but she kicked herself free.

"Get out of my way," Margaret snarled.

Snatching the rucksack, she pulled out the parachute and hobbled back towards the hatch.

"Goodbye," Margaret said, clutching the handle "It's been fun but it's all over now."

"I don't think so." Jessica stood up. "You're not

going anywhere."

Kicking high, she aimed at Margaret's chin. She dodged and Jessica followed up with a roundhouse kick, striking her chest bone. Margaret staggered backwards against the door. Her hand slid into her pocket before she dived forward, slashing with a flick knife.

Jessica attempted to kick it out of her hand, but Margaret was surprisingly quick. Balancing on her good leg, Margaret lunged. White-hot pain rocketed up Jessica's arm and blood splashed on to her trainers.

"Back off or I'll aim for your artery next," Margaret warned.

Jessica stared at her trainers. *Of course!* She hadn't tried them out yet. Lifting her leg up, she snapped open the heel tag and aimed. A taser shot out, striking Margaret in the chest. She screamed as she fell to the ground, fitting violently. Her limbs stopped twitching and she lay paralysed with her eyes wide open.

"Good job," Nathan said weakly.

"It's not over yet," Jessica panted. "We have to land."

Nathan stumbled to his feet, grabbing the parachute rucksack. "Let's do it. First, we need to secure

Margaret." He ripped the taser from her and picked her up under her arms. Her head rolled forward. "She should be out for a while but we can't risk her getting the hatch open again." He dragged her back to her seat and clamped the handcuffs back on.

The Westwood girls were helping up the bodyguards but Mattie's seat was empty. Jessica ran into the cockpit. The pilot struggled to sit upright. He mumbled something to Mattie who was in the co-pilot's seat.

"We're attempting an emergency landing," Mattie said, glancing over her shoulder. "We've been given clearance to use a private airstrip. It's approaching."

Jessica gaped at her. "You can fly?"

"I used to. A long time ago."

"It's part of Westwood training," Nathan said. "You'll learn too. I'll make sure of it."

Jessica raised an eyebrow. How could he be so sure they were going to survive this? The pilot's head fell forward on to the control panel.

"He needs CPR," Mattie said. "He was complaining of chest pains. He could have had a heart attack."

Nathan threw the rucksack down. He pulled the pilot from the seat and pressed his hands against his chest, pumping up and down.

"Sit down, Jessica," Mattie said. "I need your help."

"Me?"

"Do you see anyone else about?" her grandma retorted. "I need you to monitor the altitude and airspeed as we come down. We have to get the angle of descent right." She pointed out the gauges. "Keep reading out the levels to me. We're approaching the airstrip."

Mattie clutched the throttle lever in the centre of the console. "I have to keep the nose up or we'll hit the tarmac head on."

Jessica slid into the seat and put on the set of earphones, listening to the instructions from air-traffic control. She double-checked the readings and relayed them to Mattie. Looking out the window, she could see the runway approaching.

"Oh God. Strap yourself in." Mattie pulled the throttle.

"What is it?"

"The wheels won't lower. They must have been damaged."

"Can we land without them?"

"We don't have a choice," Mattie said. "Get ready. Here goes."

Nathan strapped himself and the captain into seats.

"You need to bring the nose up more," Jessica said. "We have to hit the undercarriage, not the nose."

"So you're the expert flyer now, are you?" Mattie barked.

"I played it in a computer game at Becky's once."

Mattie pulled up as they hit the runway in a hail of sparks. The nose broke away, metal grinding. A mist of orange filled the windscreen as the plane screeched down the tarmac.

Were they on fire? Jessica heard the wail of emergency vehicles drawing closer. The plane screeched to a halt.

"Are you OK?" Mattie said, gripping Jessica's arm.

"I think so. Just about."

"Good, because your father wanted me to pass on a message." Mattie gently pushed a tendril of hair behind Jessica's ear. "He says you're grounded until you're at least eighteen."

CHAPTER
TWENTY SIX

"There's still time to back out of Westwood. I don't want you to feel under any pressure to join. Neither does Jack."

Nathan leaned back in the black leather chair in his office, deep inside MI6 HQ. The room was modern, with a large desk and sparse white walls. Jessica noticed there wasn't a single personal item like a photo lying around that revealed his personality or home life.

She took a sip of water, exhausted. She'd arrived after finishing a gruelling three-hour debriefing session with two MI6 officers. Her head ached from concentrating; she was still processing everything that had happened.

Margaret had been transferred to a high-security

prison while awaiting trial. She was planning to plead not guilty to all charges, so MI6 wanted Jessica to give evidence against her in closed court. She didn't have a problem with that if it meant that Margaret was locked up for good. Pity the same couldn't be said for Vectra. He was still at large, but plotting what exactly with the invisibility cloak? MI6 still didn't know. Now she had an "in" to find out, through joining this secret division.

"I want to join Westwood," she insisted. "I've talked it over with Dad and Mattie; they support me."

"Really? Your dad told me you'd been grounded for a month after Monaco."

Jessica flushed. "Well, sure. They weren't happy about me lying to them, of course. But they know I really want to do this and they can help me cope with the whole undercover side of things. I understand the risks; the sacrifices I'll have to make."

"I'm not sure you do," Nathan said. "You'll be living a double life. Your friends can never know what you're up to. They'll never understand what you're going through on a day-to-day basis. That puts a strain on the strongest of relationships, believe me." He took his glasses off and cleaned them with a cloth.

Jessica's relationship with Jamie and Becky had already been tested almost to breaking point this summer. Would it survive her lack of total honesty? She had no way of knowing, but she had to take the risk. It was the only way she could find out more about Sargasso and what really happened to her mum.

"I'm fine with it."

She couldn't admit her private fears to Nathan or anyone else for that matter. Dad and Mattie had enough to cope with, and were both recovering at home. MI6 had continued to pay her dad's hospital bills as promised, and he was well enough to be treated as an outpatient. Nathan had loaned them some cash to pay off the outstanding mortgage payments, but her dad was already mithering about when he could return to work.

"In that case, we need to crack on," he said briskly. "You've already signed the Official Secrets Act, right?"

"Yep." It was the first thing she'd been made to do before the debriefing. "What case are you assigning me?"

Nathan laughed. "Hold fire. Your enthusiasm's great, but it'll be a while before you're sent out into the field."

341

"I've been out in the field already in case you hadn't noticed," Jessica pointed out. "What else do I need to know?"

"Plenty. You can't rush the training. It's a steep learning curve on our programme, and not everyone makes the cut. The first six months are incredibly tough on new recruits. Only half usually make it to the next stage."

"Competition doesn't worry me." Jessica wasn't going to let someone else take her place at Westwood. There was too much at stake. "So how does this work? Do I get to miss school or is the training at weekends?"

"A mixture of weekends, after school and holidays. We try and fit it around your normal routine to avoid disrupting your studies too much. There may be times later on when you'll need to be away, coinciding with modelling assignments, of course, to keep up your cover."

"Sounds good. I can't wait to get started."

"I'm pleased to hear it." Nathan smiled. "It's going to be tough, but I'm sure you'll do well. There's another recruit starting at the same time as you, so you'll have company."

Jessica raised an eyebrow. "Anyone I know?"

"She's waiting outside. Let me get her." Nathan walked to the door and beckoned to someone.

Kat stalked in, clad in black trousers and a white shirt. Her dark hair was swept back into a ponytail; her lips painted with red gloss.

"Hello. It's so lovely to see you again." Kat smirked triumphantly.

Jessica stood up, knocking over her chair. "No way. You're letting *her* join Westwood?"

Nathan frowned. "Kat has some extraordinary talents that we wish to make use of."

"What, like being a pathological liar who's only interested in herself?" she retorted. "Are you mad? What on earth are you thinking? You can't do this."

Nathan's eyes narrowed; he looked like he was about to say something when Kat butted in.

"Mr Hall knows I'm the best choice for the job. Papa and I are now based in London and I wish to repay MI6 for its help. If it hadn't been for MI6, we could both be behind bars."

She belonged behind bars.

"I have connections all over the world; being an

Ingorokva gives me access to so many people," Kat continued. "I get to know so many things, so many interesting snippets of information. You must realize that, Jessica, right?"

Jessica glared at her. Kat wasn't exactly subtle in making her point; she had to uphold her end of the deal and not give anything away to Nathan. In return, Kat *might* tell her more about Sargasso at some point. Was this the favour she'd referred to in Monaco? That Jessica kept quiet and allowed her to join MI6? Why would someone so self-centred want to serve Her Majesty's Government and become a spy?

"Can you wait outside for a minute, Kat?" Nathan's brow furrowed.

"Of course," she said, beaming. "You're the boss."

Nathan waited until the door clicked behind her. He turned to Jessica, glaring furiously.

"Don't ever do that again," he snarled.

"What do you mean?"

"You questioned my authority in front of a fellow employee. Yes, I'm your godfather, and now your dad and I have made up, we might all get together for Sunday lunches now and then. But when you join MI6, that's where it stops. You don't get special privileges. This is a job, not a family picnic. I'll treat you like any other employee, and I demand respect and professionalism at all times. Is that clear?"

"I was just—"

"Save it," he interrupted. "I know that you don't get on with Kat but I don't care. MI6 has seen something in her that makes her an ideal recruit for Westwood. I believe that too."

Jessica's cheeks flushed. Would he still think that if he knew Kat had stolen all the valuables using the invisibility cloak, and faked her own death threats? Maybe light fingers and a devious personality were regarded as assets by MI6. Still, it was a big risk considering Mr Ingorokva's criminal connections. Kat could be playing Nathan like she'd played Jessica.

"I have to know. Will you be able to put personal feelings aside and work alongside Kat?" Nathan drummed his fingers on the table.

Jessica hesitated. Could she? It was the million-dollar question. If she said no, her invitation to join Westwood could be withdrawn and Kat would win. She had to play along and find out what she was up to.

"Of course. I'll be professional. Even around Kat."

"Good. Then we understand each other. Can you send her back in on your way out? We'll be in touch."

Jessica didn't bother saying goodbye. Was he being tough on her because he didn't want to be accused of favouritism or was he like this with everyone? She slammed the door and glowered at Kat. She looked like the cat who'd got the cream. Standing up, Kat brushed the creases out of her trousers and walked over.

"I don't get it," Jessica said. "What's in this for you? You know, Miss I-have-to-think-about-number-one."

"A chance to show my gratitude?"

"Yeah, right. That might have fooled Nathan, but not me. You're up to something. I know it."

"I have no idea what you mean," she said smoothly. "But I'm happy we're together again. Maybe we could go for a coffee after this?"

"Sorry, but there's somewhere I need to be." Jessica stalked to the lift.

"Are you going to see your boyfriend?" Kat called after her. "Or your best friend? Did you make up with her? I'm dying to know."

Jessica ignored her. She hit the lift button and stepped in. The doors closed.

Becky sat at the back of the cafe, checking her mobile and sipping her favourite red-berry smoothie. Jessica weaved in between the tables, her eyes fixed on her friend. Her best friend. She shoved her hand in her pocket; she'd been picking the skin around her fingers all the way here. Now they looked like bloodied stumps.

Becky glanced up as she reached the table. Her dark bob was cut shorter and she'd had her nose pierced with a tiny gold stud.

"Thank you for agreeing to see me. I didn't expect you to come. I mean, I hoped you would." Jessica bit her lip to stop jabbering. "You're here. That's the main thing."

Smiling, Becky sprang to her feet and hugged her.

"Wow. I didn't expect that. I don't deserve it." Tears pricked her eyes.

"Sure you do." Becky pulled her hand out of her pocket and squeezed it. "Everyone needs a hug now and then, even you." She glanced at Jessica's bleeding fingers. "You won't get booked for hand modelling, you know."

"Tell me about it!"

Becky sat back down and pushed a half-eaten blueberry muffin on a plate towards her. "I saved you some."

It was like old times; they always shared their muffins. Jessica listened quietly as her friend explained how Jamie had offered to help out when Romeo was rushed to hospital with a suspected appendicitis. Carla had taken a photo of them kissing during the balcony scene.

"She sent it to you out of spite because she didn't get the role of Juliet," Becky said. "It's obvious she also fancies the pants off Jamie; not that he'd notice. You have to believe there's absolutely nothing going on between us."

"I do believe you. I'm sorry I didn't listen. I'm ashamed of myself; for everything I said."

"Don't be. It sounds like you had a rough week in Monaco."

"You could say that." Jessica nibbled on a piece of muffin. "It was hard work. Modelling can be gruelling sometimes."

This was how it'd be from now on; never opening up and being totally honest. If only she could tell Becky what had happened in Monaco. Nathan was right. This was going to be difficult.

"I believe you," Becky said. "But millions wouldn't."

"What do you mean?" Jessica frowned.

"You know, how tough can modelling really be? There's glamour, great pay and travel. What's to hate? It's like actors complaining about getting noticed in the street. It's hard to feel sympathetic when they're earning zillions of pounds."

Jessica pushed her hair behind her ears. "You're right. I should quit griping. I'm lucky. How—?" She hesitated, playing with the sugar cubes. "How is Jamie these days?"

"You haven't seen him since you got back?"

She shook her head. "I was too embarrassed after the way I behaved. He must think I'm raving mad."

"He doesn't. He talked about you constantly while you were away."

"What? Even when all his groupies were around? I saw the pictures from the gig."

"He didn't encourage it," Becky insisted. "But you're probably going to have to get used to fans hanging around if you're going to be with him. His band's amazing. They could be big one day. He's a gorgeous god of love, remember?"

Jessica burst out laughing. "Have you told Jamie that's your nickname for him?"

Her friend shuddered. "Like I'd admit to that. Seriously though, Jessica – go see him. Tell him how you feel."

"I can't. Not after accusing the two of you of being involved."

"I never told Jamie about any of that," Becky said. "He has no idea."

"Did I mention that I don't deserve you?"

"You owe me one," she said, finishing her drink. "His band's doing rehearsals near here. I thought we could head over there and watch."

"What, *now*? Like this? I haven't even dressed up." Jessica cast a look over her black jeans, T-shirt and jacket.

"You look sickeningly good, as usual. Come on. We can catch a bus down the street." She grabbed her hand. "Let's go."

*

Jessica's stomach lurched as Becky pushed open the door to the hall.

"Hold on a second," she said, taking a deep breath. Her palms were sweaty and she could swear she was having palpitations. "OK. Let's do this."

Becky held the door open for her, as guitars and drums belted out. "Let me know how it goes." She gave Jessica a quick peck on the cheek.

"You're not coming?" Jessica was gripped with panic.

"I thought I'd give you both chance to catch up. You've got a lot to talk about."

"But—"

"See you!" Becky waved and walked briskly away.

Jessica hesitated. She was dying to see Jamie but did he want to see her? Could she compete with his devoted fans? She walked in, her heart beating rapidly. Jamie was centre stage, strumming his guitar alongside his bandmates. He was as drop-dead gorgeous as ever, with dishevelled blond hair and a light tan. His checked shirt clung to his biceps as he played.

Looking up, a lopsided grin crept across his face. Jessica's knees weakened and her cheeks turned scarlet; the way they always did around him. It was *so* embarrassing. One look from those stunning blue eyes and she was reduced to a gibbering wreck. He'd better not come over to talk just yet; she wouldn't be able to get any words out. Her mobile vibrated. Without taking her eyes off Jamie, she fumbled in her bag. It was probably Becky, double-checking that she hadn't chickened out.

Well, she hadn't; not yet anyway.

Jessica glanced down, frowning. She didn't recognize the number. It'd better not be from Carla. She'd kill her if she tried to cause more trouble with Becky and Jamie. No way would she let her drive a wedge between them all again. Opening the text message, she gasped. She had no idea who it came from; it contained just four words.

Sargasso. Come alone. Now.

LOOK OUT FOR JESSICA'S
FIRST THRILLING MISSION...

SARAH SKY

JESSICA COLE
MODEL SPY

CODE RED LIPSTICK

Fashion Assassin is Sarah Sky's second novel in the JESSICA COLE: MODEL SPY series. Sarah is a freelance education journalist and a fan of martial arts. She is currently training for her black belt in karate after getting her brown belt/two white stripes and has a green belt in kick-boxing. She lives in London with her husband and two young children. She would have loved to become a spy but was never recruited by MI6. Or was she…?

@sarahsky23